MW00937384

Into the Shadows

Copyright © 2018 Brian Gibson

CHAPTER 1

David rode his bike across the open field next to the old water treatment plant and down an incline into a wooded area known as The Shadows. He walked his bike through the woods until he reached the riverbank. David laid his bicycle down and looked out over the swiftly flowing water that had swallowed his father and brother. A few weeks prior they had embarked on a fishing trip on the wide river and had never come back.

After two days of dredging the murky water, the police discovered the corpse of David's father among the thick reeds of the shoreline a mile downriver. Another two weeks of searching came up with nothing, and they had called it off. Sam Collie was officially listed as a missing person, although it was an unspoken foregone conclusion that he had drowned. Soon after, David started to ride his bike down to The Shadows and walk along the water's edge. He always ended up in the same spot looking out over the river, wondering.

On today's excursion David's wandering ended at a different spot by the water. He found himself standing on a drainage pipe that fed into the river from the water treatment plant. David stood on the big metal cylinder that jutted out from some tall grass and gazed out on the river. He admired the scenery and breathed in the unmistakable smell of riverbank mud.

As David was about to head home, he looked down and saw a string floating out from the pipe. Curious and compelled by a strange feeling, he knelt down and pulled on the string. Finding it caught on something, he tugged on the string a few more times, but it barely budged. Now he was really curious. David laid stomach down on the pipe to see what it was attached to. Maybe someone had hidden something in the pipe. He hung his head down and looked into the pipe, trying to keep his hair from touching the water.

2

Immediately, he jolted his head back, almost falling into the water, gasping at the startling sight. The string he was pulling on was the untied and frayed shoelace of his brother's sneaker. Sam's body floated face up surrounded by trash that had collected inside the metal tube. David froze with shock. He did not cry, but just stared at the grim discovery he had made. Although this was surely to be the darkest day of his life, David calmly got up and made his way out of the woods to go tell his mother.

David would never forget that afternoon of October 10, 1982. But instead of being afraid of The Shadows, he had become irresistibly drawn to that area.

Four years later, David faced the three bullies in front of him. Brock Shills, Sean Silver, and Joe Follson continually menaced him. Most of his peers at school viewed David as an outcast because he was a loner. All David desired was to be left alone to live a normal life like other teenagers.

Brock, a tough junior mounted David's bike and rode it around in circles to taunt him.

"Get off my bike, you jerk."

Brock hopped off the bike and threw it to the ground, which was mostly gravel and patchy grass. "What are you gonna do about it?" He advanced on David and shoved him to the ground.

David sat up and examined his scraped and bloody elbows. He shouted to the woods on his left, "You coming out here to help me?"

Brock gestured dismissively. "There ain't no one with you, Collie. Stop stalling and get up so I can beat your ass."

David nodded to the woods. "There's someone there." The bully smirked and shook his head.

"Take a look for yourself if you don't believe me."

The three boys traded quizzical squints, then moved closer to the brush to check out David's claim. Sean cautiously pushed aside a branch at the threshold of the woods and the three gazed in. They saw nothing but a dead muskrat pinned to the earth with a stick in the middle of a small clearing.

Suddenly, a rock whizzed through the leaves of the old leaning trees and Brock was struck in the head. He yelped and dropped to his knees as the other two instinctively searched for the attacker. They soon turned their attention to David, who still sat on the ground.

"Don't look at me. I told you I wasn't alone."

Sean and Joe picked up Brock, now bleeding from his wound. He rose woozily. They supported him and hurried away as David retrieved his bike and pushed it toward the woods. He watched the two boys and their wobbly leader head across the field to the access road behind the water treatment plant. David hunted for his friend.

"Now you did it! You know I'm going to get blamed for this!" There was no reply.

It was almost five o'clock, time to head home. He thought the long way through the woods was probably his best bet, just in case one of the boys was waiting for him behind the plant. They probably had taken Brock home by now, but he didn't want to chance it. He shouted into the woods, "Well, thanks for saving me, Patrick, even though you probably got me in trouble!" As he started to ride his bike down the trail, he glanced back and muttered, "Wherever you are."

The ominous timbered area known as The Shadows had gotten its name from the locals for different reasons and rumors. Freight train tracks ran straight through the town, sliced into the woods, and crossed over the river. A decade earlier, two high school sweethearts had made a suicide pact and finalized it when they stepped out onto the tracks in front of an oncoming freight train. Since then there had been recurring stories of seeing the doomed lovers wandering the area at night. Not many people frequented these woods anymore, but David considered The Shadows his sanctuary.

David shot out of the brush on his bike and raced home hoping to avoid his mother nagging him due to his tardiness. Ten minutes later, he dropped his bike in the backyard and went in through the back door. His stepfather settled at the kitchen table, having just gotten home from work. The two of them did not talk much even though his mother had been married to Steve for two years now. With conversation strained between them, David did what he could to avoid it completely. Some days Steve tried with David, and other days he just left him alone, not making any effort with his hostile stepson. David did not like the thought of someone taking the place of his father. He despised the fact that his mother had the new last name of Mathis. It felt like she was betraying his father.

His mother was just finishing cooking dinner. "David, please try to be home a little earlier. You know I don't like you out past five on a weekday, especially when you're almost late for supper."

"Yeah, I know, Mom, I know," David replied, blowing off her comments as he walked through the kitchen.

"Listen to your mother, David," Steve chimed in as he sat at the kitchen table reading the paper. Rolling his eyes, David tried to make his way upstairs, but his mother insisted that he just wash up at the kitchen sink. Beth Collie Mathis tried to keep her son close to her and her husband as much as she was able. She knew if David went upstairs, he would take as much time as he could to shorten his time at the dinner table with his stepfather. While David was washing his hands, Beth noticed the scratches on his elbows and dirt on his jeans.

"David, what happened to you?"

"Ah, I just fell when I was in the woods." His mother took another glance at the raw scratches and went back to putting the food out on the table.

5

Dinner was the same as usual with David hastily eating his meal to be able to leave the table as soon as possible. His mother asked the same routine questions hoping David would open up one of these times.

"So, what did you do today at school?"

David played with his food. "Nothing interesting really. Just a bunch of the same."

The teen continued to evade his mother's mundane questions, bolting the rest of his pork chops and abruptly leaving the table without even excusing himself.

Upstairs he changed out of his clothes and lay on his bed thinking about what had happened with Brock. His mind wandered over the possible consequences that might stem from the event. The anxiety of the day had tired David out, and he soon drifted off into a restless sleep.

CHAPTER 2

He woke up blinking and glanced over at his alarm clock. It read 7:17 p.m. David got off his bed, walked over to his closet, and pushed aside some flannel shirts. He removed a wooden panel from the back of his closet and lifted a shoebox from the compartment he had constructed. This was one of the few things he really enjoyed. He made his way to the seat next to his window.

As he sat down and opened the shoebox, he heard a knock at the front door. His mother greeted the visitor, and he heard his stepfather's heavy footsteps cross the dining room floor into the living room. He strained to listen as Steve spoke to the stranger. An unfamiliar voice said, "Sorry to interrupt your evening, folks, but I'm here to talk to your son."

"David, come down here, please," his mom called up the steps to him. He placed the lid back on the shoebox and returned it to the secret compartment. He could hear the conversation continue, but could not make out the words.

"No, it's fine, really. David!" his mother called again. As he slowly walked down the stairs, David saw the concern on his mother's face. "From what you have told us, officer, I understand that maybe David can help clear some things up."

All three adults turned their attention to David as he entered the room. Beth said, "David, this is Officer Keller. He would like to ask you some questions."

"Do you know why I'm here?"

David looked up at the man. "Kind of." Steve walked out of the room shaking his head.

Beth led her son to the couch and sat down next to him. Officer Keller remained standing.

"A boy named Brock Shills had to go to the hospital today to get his temple stitched up after he was hit with a rock. His two friends helped him back to his house since he was also slightly concussed. Both he and his two friends think David threw the rock that hit him."

Beth looked confused. "What do you mean they think David threw the rock?"

"Well, ma'am, that's why I'm here, to get this cleared up. I came to see what David has to say." The policeman looked over at David and waited for the boy to speak.

"It all happened fast," David said. "I was down by the woods just hanging out, and these three kids from my school showed up. They knew I'd be there, since I am most days."

"Did they go down there to look for you?" the officer asked.

Beth put her hand on her son' s shoulder. "David, look at me. You should not be going down there at all. If something ever happened to you in those woods, God forbid, no one would be around to help you. Now, what's wrong with these kids that they would come and find you?"

David looked down at the orange shag carpet. He knew he had to explain how this all came to be in order to get this interrogation over with. "Sean Silver, Joe Follson, and Brock Shills all hang out together. There have been some incidents at school that I don't really want to get into, but they treat me different just because I am who I am."

David paused as the officer kept his unflinching eyes on the teenager. "Earlier today at school something happened, and I finally said something back. I could only take it for so long."

The officer looked at Mrs. Mathis. "Did you know this was going on at school? Sounds like your son is being bullied."

"He doesn't really like to talk about school, so I leave him alone about it for the most part rather than get him upset." She turned to her son. "But David, you know you can come to me about things like this. I can talk to your school to make sure this stops."

—

8

"It doesn't matter, Mom, I'm used to it, but when it gets bad I can handle it."

Beth's voice started to crack as she spoke. "David, I..."

Officer Keller interrupted. "Not to be rude, but I came here to sort out this rock throwing situation involving the Shills boy. I'm not trying to be insensitive, but I have to do my job in order to finish my report."

Beth looked at David with brimming eyes. "I understand, officer. I apologize, but I had no idea this was happening at school."

David sighed. "Well, I guess you can call Brock the leader of that group. They usually say things to me and push me around sometimes." His mother gasped as she held back tears. David ignored his mother and continued. "But I know how to get back at them since I can sense some things about them."

This kid was turning out to be one of the stranger ones the now confused officer had come across in recent memory.

"Today Brock shoved me against my locker as he walked by. I just said to him, 'Do you like beating on me like your father does to you?' Well, he didn't like that too much. I guess he was embarrassed since there were other kids around, so he turned and started towards me like he was gonna do something. But he just said 'You'll get yours later'."

The officer had heard about numerous incidents of students getting picked on at school, and he felt for David, but right now he just wanted to put this situation to rest. "So what happened then?"

David took a deep breath. "Well, I was down there with my friend playing around in The Shadows, and those two other guys came down with Brock. I came out of the woods to grab my bike so they wouldn't take it, and that's when Brock started with me. Before I could get to my bike, Brock picked it up and started to ride it around, mocking me. When I told him to get off, he threw it down, charged at me and knocked me to the ground. I warned them I had a friend in the woods, hoping they would back off, but they didn't believe me. When they went to look for themselves, Brock was hit with the rock."

The officer looked at David. "Did you throw the rock, David?"

"It wasn't me. I told those guys it wasn't me, but since they didn't see no one else they blamed me, I guess."

Officer Keller appeared frustrated. "Then who was it? Was it this 'friend'? Who is he? Or it is a she?"

David squirmed a little on the couch and looked away from the officer. "It's a he...a guy. He's a friend...sort of." Beth looked surprised. "But he doesn't go to our school. His name is Patrick. I don't know his last name."

"So, he threw the rock, then? Is that what you're saying? Patrick did it?" the officer asked.

David took a few seconds before answering. "He was in the woods, and I don't know where he was at that exact moment, so all I can tell you is that it was not me."

Beth turned to her son. "How do you know this Patrick?"

"I only know him because he goes down there by himself like I do. We've talked a few times and hung out in the woods, but I don't know anything else about him."

Scratching his chin the officer looked at David's mother. "I got mixed stories from the other three boys. Brock does not remember much since that rock hit him pretty hard. Sean Silver said he didn't see David throw it, but said that Joe Follson did. However, when I asked Joe, he said he didn't see anything, but that Sean may have. I talked to all three boys separately just so I could try to get honest answers. Sounds like Sean Silver and Joe Follson never saw who really threw the rock, but were trying to get David in trouble."

The officer turned his attention to David. "As for this kid Patrick who you say was down there in the woods with you, I can't do anything about him since none of the other boys even saw him." He took a business card out of his pocket and handed it to David. "If you see Patrick there again, tell him to stop down at the station and ask for me. If he did do it, I hope he comes to his senses and confesses so we can put this to rest."

Officer Keller walked to the door and paused, looking at David. "Take care of yourself, son. Try to keep your distance from those guys. Stay away from The Shadows, too. That's not a safe area to play for a young man like you. I'd also be a little leery of making acquaintances with strangers you come across in secluded places like that. The Shadows has been known to harbor drifters."

Touching the brim of his hat the officer said, "Ma'am, thank you for your time." He walked out, and David's mother closed the door behind him, then looked over at her son.

"Why did you lie to me?" She sat heavily on the couch and put her head in her hands, crying.

Steve walked into the room, and David fled upstairs. He shut his bedroom door and flopped down onto his bed, listening to Steve trying to console his mother. What a fake Steve is, he fumed. He's nowhere to be seen when the cop is here, but comes in when he hears my mom upset so he can be the hero. He lay there trying to tune out the conversation in the living room.

David knew that he had not done anything wrong except for being in the wrong place at the wrong time. Those three have pushed me around enough. Brock had it coming to him, and hopefully he'll think twice next time, thanks to Patrick.

Meanwhile, Steve was doing his best to get Beth to see what a problem her son had become. He spelled out David's deficiencies – bad grades, no social life, and creating constant tension in the household. "You have to get tougher with him, Beth. He's using your own feelings against you."

"Steve, just give me a minute, please. I really have to think about all this." As she sat on the couch, Beth felt like a failure as a parent, and questions swirled through her mind. Did I neglect David after Charlie and Sam died? Have I drifted away from David since I got remarried? Her head throbbed.

It got quiet downstairs, and David could hear the muffled murmur of the TV in the basement. Footsteps coming up the stairs caught him off guard. Was it his mother or Steve? His bedroom was the first at the top of the steps so he did not have much time to gather himself, should whoever it was come into his room. David was already on edge from another bad day at school, followed by the incident at The Shadows. The awkward dinner, police officer's visit, and his mother sobbing downstairs only heightened his anxiety.

The footsteps paused at his door and then continued on a few more paces to the master bedroom. It was his mother – he could tell by her light step. Lying there, David knew that all he needed to do was get through Friday, and then he would have the rest of the weekend to himself. He wished that he could just fade back into being a quiet sophomore who kept to himself, but he worried that after today's incident that might never happen. Great, he thought, just something else to drive me crazy.

It was almost nine o'clock, and after the day's events, he was emotionally and physically exhausted. He turned on his side and closed his eyes. He'd had enough of this day.

CHAPTER 3

David stood facing the intimidating sight of The Shadows, when all of a sudden he saw a light shining deep in the woods. The hoot of an owl startled him as he tripped into the thick brush, chasing the light as it faded in and out, moving from left to right. What was the source? Was someone out there? The closer he walked toward the light, the farther away it seemed to get.

As David meandered through the woods, he kept his arms outstretched to feel the way as well as minding his footwork. There was only a sliver of moon and visibility was almost zero, but he was determined to discover the source of the mysterious illumination.

Then the light disappeared, leaving the teen bewildered and stopped in his tracks. His eyes strained to adjust. Which way now? He started to panic, feeling trapped, and his heart raced as he walked aimlessly, stumbling over broken branches that lay on the ground. He was not as adept as he had been a few moments earlier at moving through The Shadows. David was growing more anxious by the second when pain shot through his left knee and he doubled over. In his blindness he had walked into a boulder.

He limped as he turned around and sat on the rock to catch his breath. David looked up toward the sky, but the high canopy of The Shadows was thick, making it difficult to see the moon, let alone any stars. As he pondered his bleak situation, the place where he usually felt most comfortable, and knew so well, turned menacing.

Slumped on the rock, he suddenly heard whispers and strained to listen over the sound of chirping crickets. At first it appeared to be one voice, but then he thought he heard two. Were they the voices of the couple who died on the tracks? The voices were too soft to discern if they were male or female. As the voices became more audible, he was able to determine that one was that of a young boy and the other a man. The voices seemed to swirl around him, making him dizzy.

The young boy's voice echoed in his ears. "David...David...David..."

The older voice faded in. "David, what are you doing here? Have you come to see us?"

The younger voice, now behind him, spoke again. "David, you should not be here." The hairs stood up on his arms as his head darted from side to side in panic.

"Who is that?" David shouted out, on the brink of tears. His heart felt like it was going to beat out of his chest. "What do you want?"

"Come follow us, David. We have something you should see," the older voice said softly as it seemed to move away from him.

"How do you know my name?" he cried in panic.

The younger voice also moved away. "Come with us, David."

As David got up and started to limp forward, the woods lit up with a bright light, making it hard to see through the glare. He knew it was not from a train as there was no sound or vibration of a locomotive. The light dimmed, and once his eyes adjusted he realized that he was in an unfamiliar section of The Shadows.

David no longer heard the voices but was again blinded by the light. Just as fast as the light came on, it disappeared, making David look down and rub his eyes. He staggered and grabbed onto a tree to regain his balance, blinking his eyes to refocus. He again saw the illumination off in the distance and started walking towards it, pushing aside the thorny brush that blocked his way. His arms began to bleed from the fresh lacerations as he walked faster.

Drawing closer, David noticed a second shimmering light directly below the first. He trudged forward and the ground became softer beneath his feet. He now slipped with each step, the ground becoming muddier, then abruptly stopped when he realized he had reached the riverbank. A foghorn echoed from downriver.

Looking out over the water, he realized that the second shimmering light was just a reflection on the water of a waving flashlight. He heard the voices again, and the flashlight frantically motioned side to side in what seemed to be a distress signal. The older voice yelled out. "Hey, hey, you over there! Help us! The boat is taking on water, and my son can't swim!"

David was at a loss – he could not swim either. The older voice continued to plead, now screaming, "The rope! Grab the rope!" David looked around for a rope as the light scanned back and forth over the bank. He caught a glimpse of white just to his left as the light passed over it. Rope tied to a large piece of driftwood acted as an anchor for the small boat out on the river. David grabbed the rope and began to pull the boat toward the shore. His body ached as he exerted all his strength against the current to pull in the sinking boat. The boat began to tug David forward into the water and thick mud, and he stumbled, nearly losing his grip. He reached back, grabbing onto the driftwood with his left hand as he fell to one knee in the water.

David steadied himself and stood up, bracing his right foot on a rock, and pulled even harder. After the first few tugs, he could feel the boat start to move his way as he got into a rhythm. As the boat got closer, the man spoke. "Thank you. My son is a bit spooked right now." David could hear the sniffling of a young boy.

When the bow of the boat hit the river mud, it jerked David forward onto his hands and knees, water splashing in his face. He approached the boat awkwardly, sloshing through the waist-deep water to help the occupants disembark. The man stepped out of the boat, flashlight still in hand, and turned to grab the boy who seemed close to hyperventilating. David helped steady the boat as the young boy climbed out with his father's assistance. The boy

15

grabbed onto David's arm as he almost tumbled out of the boat. His touch was ice cold.

The young boy fell face down onto the muddy bank, prompting David to ask, "Are you okay?" There was no response from the boy except for his heavy breathing. David turned at the sound of a knife sliding from its leather sheath on the man's hip. The blade gleamed in the moonlight, and David took a step back as the man looked at him sternly.

There was nothing but silence for a few seconds. David's body tensed as the man raised the blade. He brought it down violently, making David flinch, and the big knife bit into the thick rope still anchoring the boat to the driftwood. "Help me cut this boat free. I never want to see it again," the man said in an exhausted voice.

David held the rope taut as the stranger continued to chop away, but the man soon slowed his pace as he grew fatigued. He handed David the knife. "Please, I am too tired." David took the knife and set the sharp blade on the rope where the man had been striking it. He started to cut using a sawing motion. The fibers of the rope separated one by one until he cut all the way through. David turned to hand the knife to the man whose face was in shadow. He sheathed the knife silently.

The boat was free of the rope but still stuck in the thick mud. They both started to push the boat out into the current when David felt the grasp of the man's hands under his arms. In one swift motion he was tossed into the boat. David splashed into six inches of water and his shoulder hit the hard wood seat awkwardly. The man shouted, "Now it's your turn, David!"

David sat up slowly, his shoulder aching, and looked at the man as the boat was swept out into the current. The man stood knee deep in the water, waving. "No one can survive this river. Trust me, I know." The boat began to spin slowly in the eddying water, and David felt cold panic grip him. As he lurched to his feet, the boat suddenly tilted, sending him overboard into the chilly water.

CHAPTER 4

David woke abruptly in a cold sweat and quickly sat up on his elbows, breathing heavily. The clock read 4:07 a.m. He knew he would not sleep again.

He was not the type of person to read too much into his dreams, but this one had been especially vivid. It had taken him a moment to get a grasp on what was and was not reality. Even though he could not see the faces in his nightmare, he knew they had been his dad and brother.

As he sat there, David thought about them and the rumors that had swirled in the community after that devastating incident. Questions raised on whether Charlie had drowned Sam and himself on purpose, which especially upset Beth. Others wondered why David had not been on the trip, and if there were family issues that had led up to the mishap. Instead of just accepting the accident for what it seemed to be, people tried to come up with another explanation, looking at all possible angles.

For David, the rumors at school were the toughest part of the aftermath. Sam had been more outgoing one of the two boys with the assumption being David was jealous of his brother, leading to further speculation. Their neighborhood quickly became a very uncomfortable place to live in that people talked about them more than supported the family. They had grieved in private, under a cloud of suspicion, and David grew to disdain his community.

The rumor that lingered the longest was that Steve Mathis had sabotaged the boat. Steve was good friends with David's father and was supposed to go on the fishing trip that day as well. He had come down with a stomach virus overnight and had backed out that morning. Steve had always been around to help out after the accident, but David thought he acted differently after his father was gone. It seemed like he was only there to console Beth while barely bothering with David.

Beth had struggled to make the right choices for herself and her only son. There were times when she thought of transferring David out of his elementary school, knowing he despised it. She also considered moving away from Delome, but it was not financially feasible. Besides, Beth thought moving might make it seem like they were confirming the rumors somehow. In the end, she decided to stay put just to prove to everyone that she did not care about the gossip and whispers. She wanted everyone to realize the whole tragedy was simply an accident and there was nothing to hide.

It was amazing to her that a town could treat a family so poorly when only a few years earlier it had rallied around the families of the couple who had committed suicide on the train tracks. David knew from people talking that there was a disparity in the way the town reacted to his family's plight, and he began to resent his hometown and isolate himself from everyone. When Steve and Beth took their friendship further, it reignited the rumors. The whole situation tortured David, and he often thought of running away from home.

At six o'clock in the morning, he finally decided to take advantage of his sleeplessness and get out of the house early so he would not run into his mother or Steve. He walked to the bathroom, glancing over at the closed door opposite his room, and shook his head. David's mother had pored over every inch of Sam's room after he died, clinging to any small memento she could of her son. In the end, she decided that holding on to his childhood trinkets would not bring him back. A year after his death, she cleaned out the room and changed it into an office, which went unused.

He took a quick shower, dressed and hustled downstairs. After leaving a note behind for his mom on the kitchen table, David slipped out the back door with his schoolbag slung over his shoulder. He hopped on his bike with plenty of time to himself before school started.

The teen leisurely rode through town and even cruised passed the access road that led to The Shadows. David wondered how the next couple weeks would play out in light of the Brock incident. As he was thinking about how he might handle any extra attention, he glanced at his watch and realized it was time to get to school.

As he got closer to the high school, he saw other kids on their way to the same destination. Every time he saw another schoolmate, he felt like each one was looking at him. David's paranoia increased when he walked through the school doors. He was not sure if others knew of the incident, but he did know that it would only take a few hours for the story to circulate and for David to become the most talked-about kid at school.

No one seemed to be paying attention to him walking down the hallway, which was the way he preferred it. His plan was to just make his usual rounds through the school day, acting as normal as he could manage. All he wanted was for the weekend to come and to be able to enjoy a few days off.

While being picked on for the past couple of years, David had never been involved in an incident like this. Even though he knew he had done nothing wrong, he could not do anything to stop the whispers. During his early classes he felt tense, but the first half of the day proved uneventful. As the day progressed, he felt a few more people noticed him than normal. The early word about the episode at The Shadows must have started to get around. David ignored everyone, much as he did every day, and went about his business, acting like nothing had happened.

One kid did yell out, "There's the man!" as David walked by, and he heard a group of kids talk about him as he left Chemistry class, but there was nothing much more than that. At lunchtime David walked outside to get some fresh air and avoid the whole cafeteria scene. On a routine day, he would be sitting by himself in the back of the cafeteria engrossed in a book. Today he made himself scarce under the cover of the football field bleachers. He struggled to come up with an idea to divert the attention he was garnering. He would just have to see what came next and deal with it.

After the bell sounded, David took a deep breath and went back inside to his next class. With the school day winding down, David felt relieved since it did not seem like the gossip had disseminated throughout the school as much as he anticipated. Also, knowing that the weekend was only a few classes away comforted him. The weekend would give David a couple days to figure out how he would handle any undue attention next week, as well as deal with Brock when he came back to school.

During his second to last class of the day, David stared out the window, daydreaming. Like most of the students, his teachers really did not bother with him, since asking David a question usually resulted in a shrug and silence. The class dragged on as he yearned for the day to end. He could feel his eyes starting to close, and his head nodded as he tried to keep himself awake.

When the bell rang, kids spilled out into the hallways, and David walked down the hall to his locker to grab the book for his final class. As he spun the dial on the lock, he could feel someone staring at him at very close range. Since he rarely spoke to anyone at school, David ignored the presence, hoping they would go away.

Now feeling a little nervous, he botched the combination on his lock. After another attempt, he pulled at the lock, popping it loose, and opened the green locker, throwing his English books in the top compartment. He grabbed his tattered European Studies book and positioned his body so he could make a quick getaway to avoid whomever was waiting for him. He quickly slammed the locker shut, clicked on the lock, and started to walk off. At his third stride, a voice called out, "Hey!" David rolled his eyes, disappointed that he had not made it through the end of the day without someone approaching him.

Just keep walking, he thought, looking down. Then, in a moment of clarity, he reasoned with himself. Why make this into a scene if it's just one person? Just turn around and see what they want before this lunatic starts causing a spectacle. As David turned around to face his annoyance, he met the eyes of a kid he did not recognize.

"What's up, man?" the kid said cheerfully. "My name's Luke. Just wanted to say I heard about you and Brock." The kid was just trying to show some sort of appreciation, even though David knew he had not done anything to deserve it. He walked a few steps closer to Luke, hoping to keep their conversation quiet and brief.

"It was nothing really. I didn't do anything," David replied.

"A lot of people know what happened, and some kids are glad you did it. I know I am. That piece of crap has picked on me before too. Brock has messed with a lot of people, and had it coming."

David was getting more and more annoyed, especially because the rumor apparently was that he had thrown the rock. He looked back at Luke straight-faced and raised his voice. "I'm the last person who wants people talking about any of this. Besides, I didn't do it. There was someone else there besides me and those guys." A small group of girls across the hall looked over at David strangely and whispered behind their hands.

Luke continued, "Well, whatever happened, man, there are a lot of people here that appreciate it. And I think we…"

David cut him off as the bell rang for the next class. "Listen, I have to go." David turned away and began walking down the hall, still fighting with himself for even stopping for that kid. He turned back to catch another glimpse of the person he would now try to avoid, but Luke was already gone.

He knew he would be able to relax in his last class, since his European Studies teacher was not much of a stickler. He sat down, then immediately grew anxious as he remembered that Sean Silver was in this class with him. He had been so preoccupied that he had forgotten. As the rest of the kids filed in, Sean slowly walked through the door and made steady eye contact with David as he strode across the room to his desk. The uncomfortable feeling that had slowly waned over the course of the day came back over David full force.

He did his best to pay attention to what was being taught to avoid further eye contact with Sean and to keep his mind busy. Out of the corner of his eye, David could see Sean look over a few times to intimidate him. It worked.

After the bell rang and his final class was over, David walked back to his locker with his head down, just wanting to vacate the building as soon as possible. As he was unlatching the lock, someone forcefully shouldered him from behind, causing him to drop his book and binder. He did not want to turn around, but he had a good idea of who it was. He bent down and grabbed the binder with his left hand while his right reached for the book. A foot swiftly kicked the book down the hallway.

"Watch your back, Collie," Sean muttered as he walked by. David walked over to pick up his book and saw Sean being stopped down the hall by one of the hall monitors. Mr. Gavin was a white-haired retired teacher and known as a strict disciplinarian when it came to nonsense. David could not hear most of what was being said over the noise of the crowded hall, but as Sean walked off he shrugged at Mr. Gavin as if to say, It was an accident. Mr. Gavin approached David with that recognizable limp.

"Is everything okay?"

David gathered himself. "Yeah, I'm fine."

Mr. Gavin looked him over and then stared into David's eyes. "If you have any trouble, son, you can always speak to the principal. There are people here to help you.

Me, the other hall monitor, Mr. Crandley, teachers…whoever."

David kept his head down. "Thanks. Got it."

Mr. Gavin nodded his head. "All right. Just know the help is there. Have a good weekend, Mr. Collie." As David looked up, he saw that kid Luke walking quickly away from his locker, and he caught sight of a piece of paper slipping through the vent. He lost the kid in the throng of students crowding the hallway rushing to get out of the building for the weekend. David walked over, opened his locker and looked inside, but did not see the piece of paper. Strange, he would have sworn….

Down the hall, Mr. Gavin walked into Principal Mitchell's office, closing the door behind him. After about ten minutes, Mr. Gavin walked out of the office. The principal picked up his phone, dialed a four-digit extension and waited for an answer.

"Hey, it's me. Remember the boy we discussed the other day? Well, I've been hearing some things today, and John Gavin was just in my office to tell me about a new incident. Stop by when you get a minute." Roy Mitchell hung up the phone, spun around in his chair, and looked out his window as the last few kids exited the school.

CHAPTER 5

David was in the mood to take the long way home from school. He needed to think about how he would tell Patrick that the police now knew that he was at The Shadows yesterday. Do I even tell him that they think he threw the rock? he wondered. However Patrick was going to take the news, David knew he needed to tell him.

He coasted on a downhill street and slowed to keep his distance from the pack of kids on bikes a half-block ahead of him. The last thing he wanted was for someone else to bother him or encounter any more trouble. He could feel the stress start to bubble up inside him again. All he wanted to do was get home, go upstairs and relax.

At home, Beth watched the clock, waiting for David's return. She was still concerned and embarrassed that she barely knew what was going on in her own son's life. Since she had learned yesterday how David was being mistreated at school, something had clicked in her. Beth knew she had to start making more of an effort with her son. At times over the past few years, she thought she might have acted selfishly in spending so much time with Steve and not paying more attention to David. Whatever it was, she knew today was the day that she wanted to start being more proactive in his life. She had time before Steve came home and needed to take advantage of this opportunity. She could not force David to warm up to Steve, but she could try to mend her own relationship with her son.

When David walked through the door, before he could throw his backpack on the dining room chair and head upstairs, his mother purposefully stood in his way. "Hi, David. How was your day?"

David looked at her, confused. "Fine…?"

"Hey, I was thinking we could have a talk. If you don't feel like talking, I at least want to let you know what has been on my mind…and no, it's not just about what happened yesterday."

25

David felt uncomfortable. He could blow off most people and not think twice about it, but when his mom pleaded with him, even though their relationship was not the best, he usually softened. He slumped down in a kitchen chair with his backpack resting on his lap. Beth sat in the chair across from him. He gazed at the refrigerator behind her and waited for what was about to come.

"David, I want to be as honest as possible with you. I feel that I've let you down ever since your father and brother passed. That was a very tough time for us both, and I feel like we haven't been that close ever since. I know when Steve came into the picture it pushed us further apart." Beth paused, overcome by emotion.

"As your mom, I know that I should have taken more control of our relationship, but when a family is rocked like ours was, it can confuse a person. I just want to apologize to you. When that police officer came to the house to ask you questions, I felt embarrassed. I thought I was a horrible parent for not knowing that my own son was being harassed at school. I guess that's just a part of the stupidity that came along with how I have handled our situation over the past several years."

"Mom, you don't have to do this, really."

She shook her head and her voice quivered as she went on. "I hope you know that you can talk to me about anything. I know that you may not get along with Steve, or even try to for that matter, but I'm not going to force you to do anything you don't want to. The only thing I ask is to be more open with me and let me know what's going on in your life. This incident has really opened my eyes, and for the first time in a while I am seeing things more clearly."

Beth now had tears rolling down her cheeks as she stared at her son sitting across from her. "I guess I have been holding this in for a long time, but I did not want to upset you. Or for you to feel like I am bothering you with my own feelings…I don't know…I am just so sorry."

26

David felt he needed to say something even though it was tough for him, since his mother had just poured out her emotions. "I'm fine with everything, Mom, really I am. It's been tough for us, but it will get better. And I'll try to be better on my side of things." He stood up and she wrapped him in a hug for a few seconds. She watched as he walked into the dining room, put his schoolbag down on the chair, and made his way upstairs.

David shut his bedroom door, leaned against it, and took a deep breath. It was a relief to be back in his room. Did she really think she could make up for years of neglect with a three-minute heart to heart? He walked over to his bed and fell face down into his pillows.

Forty-five minutes later he woke up with his head still stuffed in the pillows but not feeling much better. He knew what would help ease his mind. He pushed himself up and walked to the closet where he removed the hidden shoebox. He sat in the seat by his window, opened the box, and stared at the contents inside for a moment. Yes, this always helped.

There was a sudden knock at the door, which startled him, and he hurried to slide the shoebox under his bed. When he opened the door, Steve was standing there with a blank look on his face. "Your mother wanted me to come get you for dinner. She called for you, but I guess you didn't hear her."

David looked coldly into Steve's eyes. "I'll be there in a minute." He closed the door and sat on his bed for a minute, knowing that his interactions with Steve will always be uncomfortable. Neither of them ever made much of an effort with the other. He could not pinpoint exactly why, but he had felt suspicious of Steve ever since the accident.

He knelt down to grab the shoebox from under his bed to put it back in its hiding place. He had slid the box farther under his bed than he thought and had to lie on the floor to reach it. With his head next to the vent, he heard Steve murmur something to his mom in the kitchen.

Beth replied, "Just give him time, Steve, he'll come around eventually."

"It's been two years already, how much more time does he need? He's a lost cause in my mind at this point, Beth."

Beth sighed and shook her head.

David's anger flared at what he had just heard, especially knowing he had to go down there to eat dinner with Steve to appease his mother. He got ahold of the shoebox, walked it over to the closet, and shoved it back in the compartment, covering it with the wooden panel. He slowly walked down the stairs, annoyed. He would just have to keep his temper in check and pretend he had not heard the exchange. The smell of lemon-pepper chicken filled the house as he turned the corner into the dining room and walked into the kitchen. He sat down without saying a word.

Beth greeted him with a smile on her face, "David, I made a little extra mac and cheese for you tonight. I figured you'd like it after the tough week you've had."

David looked up at his mom and muttered, "Thanks." He knew his mother was trying her hardest to get more involved in his life and make up for lost time. Although he did not understand why she hadn't tried harder a few years back, David recognized he could be a difficult kid.

As they passed around the food, there was the usual awkward silence. When Steve was running late, Beth would wait for him to eat while David would just have supper in the basement or his bedroom alone. Occasionally, David would opt to stay in his room by pretending to not feel well or just sleep through dinnertime. Either way, he would rather pull leftovers out of the fridge and eat by himself in his room if he had the choice.

Starting a conversation always seemed difficult at the dinner table. Beth felt it was her duty to create some sort of dialogue with the two men in her life. If she was desperate, she would try an easy icebreaker like talking about the weather or an anecdote from her workday. Steve was apprehensive about initiating a conversation since he knew David disliked him. David knew his stepfather did not understand him, but he did not have time for fake people like Steve. Now with his mom trying to repair things between them, which included somehow bringing David and Steve closer together, the uneasiness was palpable.

After everyone began eating, Beth was about to open her mouth when surprisingly Steve decided to start up some discourse. "How was school today, David?"

A couple of thoughts passed through David's mind at this halfhearted attempt. Who does this guy think he is? Does he think I'm stupid or that I can't see right through him? David started to answer, then hesitated. He wanted to scream every expletive he could think of at his stepfather. He looked at Steve across the table and plainly said, "What do you care?"

Steve dropped his fork onto his plate and threw his hands in the air. "I give up!" he shouted. He grabbed his wallet off the counter, snatched his keys from the key rack, and walked out the door. In an instant Beth's excitement at a new beginning with David dissolved. The sound of a car door opening and slamming shut could be heard clearly inside the house. The car started up and then hurriedly backed out of the driveway onto the street.

Beth looked at her son. "Why don't you just give him a chance?"

David looked at his mother, feeling he owed her some justification. "I guess I'm just a lost cause at this point."

29

CHAPTER 6

David's week had not gotten any better, and he wondered if it could get any worse. He had been waiting for this for the last couple of days, just being by himself in his room, not having to worry about school the following day. His mother, the police, and some kids at school knew that someone else might have been with him at The Shadows during the Brock run-in. Most people did not believe David, but he knew Patrick had to have thrown the rock. As he lay on his bed his anxiety increased. He had to tell Patrick people were aware he was down there and that the police wanted to speak with him.

Maybe if Patrick just lay low for a while until this all blew over, everything would be fine. There was really no way to cover it up; it was because of David that the police knew about Patrick. The good thing was he had barely told that police officer anything about him. After all, David himself did not know much about Patrick, even his last name for that matter. He would just have to go to The Shadows tomorrow and let Patrick know what had transpired over the last twenty-four hours.

David glanced around his room, which was much more simplistic than most teenage boys'. There was no video game console, no television, and no stereo. He had a bookcase stuffed with his reading materials, mainly comics, books of science fiction, horror and fantasy, and several outdated outdoor magazines his father used to subscribe to. David did not have much interest in sports or have many hobbies – those had died when half his family did.

He had a few porcelain animal miniatures on a shelf above his dresser. A nightstand next to his bed had his alarm clock on top along with the book he was currently reading. A box of tissues and a note pad, which he used to write down his nighttime thoughts, occupied the second shelf of the nightstand.

He stretched over to grab his book from the nightstand and fanned through the pages until he reached the dog-eared page halfway through marking the last section he had read. Whether getting lost in a book, passing time in his room, or hanging out down at The Shadows, David sought solace by escaping from people. After taking in about twenty pages, David laid the book next to him on the bed and closed his eyes.

After what seemed like only a few minutes, David awoke from his sleep, startled. He rolled over, reaching for the phone on the floor. At that same moment, Beth was coming up the steps and slowed as she got to her son's closed bedroom door. She heard David talking and stood there, eavesdropping. Beth turned, shaking her head, and made her way across the hall to her bedroom.

"OK, we'll meet up soon if you'll be around. Sounds good, Aaron. Talk to you later." David placed the receiver back in the cradle and immediately fell back to sleep.

The next day David got up around nine-thirty and went downstairs to get himself some breakfast. Steve was still in bed reading the paper as he usually was on Saturday mornings, while his mom was at the breakfast table drinking her coffee. David knew she would want to discuss the incident from last night and would probably start in on him as soon as he walked into the room. Before the conversation even began, David cut her off, saying, "I'm okay, Mom. Don't worry about it."

Beth knew not to patronize her son, so she did not want to come on too strong. "I just want you and Steve to feel comfortable with one another. Maybe you will understand each other someday."

David, wanting to avoid the subject, just nodded in agreement and poured himself some cereal. On this morning he decided it would be best to oblige his mother in conversation. He was well aware she appreciated times like this with him since they did not have very many of them.

31

The guileful teen knew when to appease his mother, which in turn meant she would lay off him for a while. Even a kid as cold as David had something of a soft spot for his mother, but he still knew how to play to her emotions. Some small talk ensued as he slurped up the rest of his cereal and drank the milk out of the bowl.

Now that he was back in his mom's good graces, he felt that he had earned some well-deserved time to himself and would take advantage of it. Back in his room he grabbed a backpack from his closet and stuffed some useful objects in it for his day down at The Shadows, as his father had always taught him to be prepared. Whether Patrick was down there or not, David wanted to alert him any way he could, even if that just meant leaving him a note. He did not want to see Patrick get in trouble because of something he had blurted out while under the pressure of police questioning.

He slung the backpack over his shoulder as he headed downstairs and yelled to his mother in the basement to let her know he was leaving. He hopped on his bike and sped down the driveway anticipating an enjoyable, quiet ride through his neighborhood. He looked at the houses that occupied his block and observed a few neighbors out completing some morning chores, like mowing the lawn and gardening. A few people had taken advantage of the unseasonably warm morning and sat on their front porches reading the paper.

The Shadows was about a fifteen-minute ride, mostly downhill, from David's house. He took his time getting there, because he was a little nervous to talk with Patrick, but at the same time he did not want to avoid the situation any longer and possibly make matters worse for his friend.

David veered off the street onto a dirt path that led to one of the many trails into the wooded area. As he had been told by his mother and the police officer not to go to The Shadows, he would have to be careful. He brushed past some hanging branches and jumped off his bike, holding onto the handlebars to jog beside it. The large roots that swelled from the ground along with the scattered about rocks made the terrain too tough to ride over.

After a few minutes of walking his bike through the woods, he reached a small clearing and leaned his bike pedal against a rock that served as a kickstand. David sat on the large trunk of a fallen tree and took in his surroundings. He had met up with Patrick at this spot before and hoped today would be no different. Patrick and David spent many hours here at The Shadows. They would hunt small animals like squirrels, groundhogs or the occasional muskrat, or travel around the woods searching for new spots or nooks they hadn't been to before.

Recently, while deep in the woods by himself, David thought he saw a makeshift campsite with a blue tarp draped over some branches, but it had been almost dark and he could not tell, even by using his binoculars. Being alone, David did not want to venture any closer and quickly left, a little spooked. It had been a few weeks since he had made that observation and had kept away from that location. Since then, each time he had come to The Shadows, he got the feeling that someone was watching him.

After waiting a while, David found himself lying on his back with his mind starting to wander. He stared at the canopy above him and let his eyes close. Suddenly, he thought he heard something or someone rustling in the brush. David quickly sat up and looked around. He did not see anyone, but it was easy to hide in a densely wooded area such as this. He looked at the watch attached to his bag and saw that it was about one forty-five. Figuring Patrick was not going to show up, David decided he would just leave him a note at another spot they both frequented – the drainpipe where he had found his brother's body.

David had taken Patrick to that spot once he had gotten to know him and felt comfortable, believing Patrick was someone he could trust. In a way, he felt telling the story of finding his brother's corpse would win him respect. After hearing about his family's misfortune, David's friend informed him he also had gone through something similar. The girl who had committed suicide on the freight train tracks with her boyfriend was Patrick's sister. From that day on, David and Patrick had a connection.

David made his way to the southeast section of The Shadows, convincing himself that leaving a note was the right thing to do. Since he had first brought Patrick down to the drainpipe, David would sometimes find him sitting on it looking out over the river. As David headed toward his destination, he started to get an uneasy feeling as if someone were following him.

He picked up his pace, glad he had left his bike behind so it did not slow him down. He was getting more and more paranoid with each step and kept his head on a swivel. He could see the clearing in the distance and began to jog towards it, thinking he could hear someone tracking him from behind. David could not help but remember his dream with the ghostly voices. His jog turned into a run, and his heart started to beat faster. As he neared the clearing, his foot hit a tree root and he fell forward, sliding onto the dirt. David rolled over and grabbed his right ankle while wiggling off his backpack. He rolled back and forth on his back and groaned in agony.

After a few minutes, the pain subsided and he hobbled to his feet, bracing himself on a tree. He looked around, but did not see anyone. If someone were after me they had the perfect chance to get me, he reasoned. He wondered if Patrick had been following him or if it had been anyone at all.

David limped around in a small circle to get his ankle loose and work out the soreness. He knew that Patrick was either in the woods avoiding him or would be there at some point, since he was almost always there on Saturdays. David pulled out the notepad and pen as he approached the pipe, thinking of how he could best summarize his talk with the officer. He sat down on the rusty metal and began putting his thoughts on paper to explain the situation to Patrick. David implored him to be careful in The Shadows now that the police knew about him. The blare of the freight train horn interrupted his concentration, and he watched it cross the bridge, rumbling its way south.

He signed the letter, cautiously walked out towards the end of the pipe, and placed it in a rusted-out cavity with a rock on top. David headed back into the woods to retrieve his bike, but for good measure he took a different route, still a little shaken. A moment later, a man stepped out of his hiding spot in the bushes and walked over to the pipe. He reached down and removed the rock that weighed down the note and unfolded the paper, squinting as he read it. He looked in the direction that David had taken and shook his head. Then he replaced the note along with its paperweight and jumped off the pipe, jogging after David.

CHAPTER 7

David's ankle began to throb again as he jogged up a small incline into the thicker brush, but he was able to tolerate it. Although he came down to The Shadows regularly and had familiarized himself with most of this wooded landscape, he had not frequented this section very often. Soon he became disoriented and was not sure which direction would take him back to his bike. Maybe it was nerves or the paranoia that someone had followed him, but he was definitely feeling lost.

He kept on moving forward through the brush when after a few minutes he stumbled into a campsite. It had to be the same place he had seen before with the binoculars. He recognized the blue tarp. There was nobody around, and David's curiosity got the best of him as he moved the blue tarp aside with the back of his hand to get a look behind it.

A dented metal pot, some canned goods, a sleeping bag, toilet paper, and a rusty fork were some of the items he noticed right away. An old beat-up shopping cart sat off to the side with a shovel and some rope inside. David wondered about the effort it must have taken to get it this deep in the woods.

As he scanned the bunk area, he noticed another folded tarp lying noticeably out of place. David picked up the tarp, which revealed a small chest in a hole dug into the ground. The lock on the chest was not fastened, and David reached to open it knowing he was grossly invading someone's privacy, but he could not help himself.

Just as his hand touched the chest, he heard something stirring in the bushes a short distance behind him. He quickly looked over his shoulder and steadied himself with his hands on the ground. He saw a head with finely groomed brown hair trying to duck behind a short shrub. Definitely not Patrick. Maybe the owner of the campsite? In an instant David pushed off the ground from his squat and took off in the opposite direction of the man. He felt his backpack bobbing from side to side as he ran. His ankle ached with every stride, but he was in panic mode and his adrenaline had taken over. So he wasn't just paranoid – someone had been following him.

After running a stretch as fast as the wooded terrain would allow, he realized the man did not appear to be following him anymore. David slowed down, then finally paused for a moment, taking in his surroundings. He had finally entered a location he was familiar with. After a short hike he had his bike, and as soon as he reached level ground, he jumped on, pedaling fast as the grass turned into asphalt, separated by a crumbled curb. Now he knew he was safe. He coasted by a lone white car with a peace sticker on the bumper. That was weird. Nobody ever parked there, and he had never seen that car around before.

While riding home he thought about the person who had been following him in the woods. David had no idea who it could have been, but there was no way a homeless person living in The Shadows would have hair that well-kept. But who else could it be?

David rode up his driveway at 4:30 p.m. It was one of the few times in recent memory that he was glad to be home. Steve's car was not there, which came as a relief. He found the back door locked, which meant that his mom and Steve had gone out. Thank God, he thought as he swung his backpack around to retrieve his key. He walked through the doorway tossing his keychain with enough force to slide across the counter and hit the backsplash.

He saw a note held to the fridge by a "Sunny Florida" palm tree magnet.

David, Steve and I went out to dinner and a movie. There is a Salisbury steak TV dinner in the freezer. Be back later on. Love, Mom

Taking into account the drive, David knew he would have the next several hours to himself. Perfect.

David's house was one of the few in his neighborhood with a finished basement, which doubled as their family room. He chuckled to himself whenever he thought of it as the family room since his family was anything but that at the present time. He walked carefully down the basement steps with the hot meal fresh from the microwave in his left hand and a cup of orange soda in the other. He placed his dinner on the table and sat back on the couch waiting for it to cool down. He gazed around the basement in disgust. It had been transformed from his dad's sanctuary into Steve's room all too fast in David's mind. Sports memorabilia had replaced all the pictures of wild game and mounted animal heads David's dad had hunted. Even though Steve and Charlie had been friends, David could not understand their friendship knowing what he did now about Steve.

His stepfather had also hung up some sports mementos from his high school playing days, which David found to be pompous. I would love to tear all this crap off the walls, he thought. David turned on the television and picked up the channel changer box, which had a cord connected to the TV. He put the box on the table in front of him next to his meal and started to eat. David felt like he was invading Steve's space whenever he was in the basement even though he had lived in this house his entire life. He felt uncomfortable and rebellious at the same time while down here, especially when he chose to sit in Steve's recliner.

He looked over at Steve's framed high school football jersey on the wall as he took a bite of his dinner. Steve had led his team to victory in the state championship as quarterback during his senior season, and the jersey was special to him. When Steve and his mom had first gotten together, he had shared many high school sports stories with David, looking to impress him. But David showed no interest in sports, popularity, or what others thought of him, and the stories just underscored how shallow Steve was.

Soon after Steve realized he was not dazzling the teen with tales of high school grandeur, he did not try as hard with him. That idiot probably would have picked on me in high school if we had been in at the same time, David thought.

He took his eyes off the number 13 jersey and scooped up some potato that accompanied the Salisbury steak dinner. He flipped through some channels and stopped on a station with President Reagan giving a speech about something political David did not understand. He clicked off the TV and pushed the empty cardboard shell from his dinner aside.

After a minute he got up and walked over to the door that led into a back room of the basement. The ever-present smell of mildew hit him in the face. The back room of the basement did not have many visitors, and the contents of the boxes explained why.

He walked into the dark a couple of feet and reached up to feel for the string that hung from the only light fixture. He tugged it too hard, causing the string to snap. David stumbled into the boxes and one hit the cement floor with a loud thud. He flipped over a milk crate, spilling the contents, and used it as a stepstool to reach the broken string and turn on the light, which revealed the mess he had made on the floor. He stepped off the crate and began to gather the binders and strewn about paperwork. As he was stuffing the contents back into the fallen box, he noticed just how moldy some of the cardboard boxes on the bottom of the pile had become.

Black mold ran up the walls, caused by the water that seeped into this part of the basement through the cinderblock. It was depressing for David to see just how neglected these boxes had been, since they stored the belongings of his father and brother.

Over the next few hours, he sat on the crate and pored over the old photographs, paperwork, writings, school papers, and other items. David read a few short stories his brother had written and even came across a few of his own that were somehow mixed in. Sam had also been a good artist as evidenced by the drawings that David was admiring. He flipped through some paintings of nature scenes and wild animals, which his brother had enjoyed doing most.

David came upon a footlocker at the bottom of one pile, knowing he should push this one off to the side and resist the urge to sift through it. Some boxes brought back memories more vividly than others, such as the box of poems his father had written, which he used to read to the boys at night. David read one fishing poem and muttered the last two lines aloud. It was one of his favorites. Whenever you don't catch a fish, and the end of the day is near, look forward to fishing tomorrow, and remember I'll always be here. How ironic that his father was gone because of a fishing accident.

He exhaled and leaned back as he looked up at the joists and ductwork covered in old, dusty gray cobwebs. And then he did something he had not done in a long time. The boy who many thought had no emotion allowed tears to stream down his face for a minute before he wiped them away with the sleeve of his green flannel shirt. David put the poem back in its binder and sifted through a different box that held some of his brother's old toys and school pictures.

After realizing that he had been in the basement for close to four hours, he started cleaning up. He did not want to be downstairs when his mother and Steve returned, and he rushed to get things back in order. He reached for the broken string to turn out the light and glimpsed at the other half that lay on the cold floor. He thought for a moment, his hand in midair, then grabbed the string on the ground. He stood on the corners of the milk crate again and tied the two pieces of string back together. "I'll be back. I promise," he said aloud. He pulled on the string to shut off the light and smiled. David closed the door and grabbed the remnants of his dinner. As he jogged up the stairs, he paused and looked back down at the room that Steve had taken over, shaking his head.

CHAPTER 8

Back in his room, David was happy he had made it upstairs before his mother and Steve came back, so he did not have to feign conversation. After he finished getting ready for bed, he closed his bedroom door, grabbed his book, and lay down with his alarm clock glowing 10:38 p.m. No more than five minutes later, a car pulled into the driveway. David jumped up and turned off his bedroom lights to give the illusion that he was sleeping so no one bothered him. The teen was always prepared for the dark with the flashlight and candles he kept under his bed. He heard the back door open and keys hit the floor as heavy footsteps clumsily walked across the kitchen. He heard his mom laugh at something Steve said and then let out a hiccup. "I love you, babe," she giggled.

David cringed. I hope she's been drinking to be acting that way.

Then he heard Steve, sounding slightly intoxicated, ask, "How about one more glass, dear?" David heard the clink of wine glasses being removed from the cabinet and the pop of a wine cork. He could hear murmured conversation in the living room. After about a half-hour, he heard Steve say, "All right, it's bedtime for us. I can see you're definitely ready." They made their way upstairs, passing by David's room without stopping. It did not take long before he heard deep, even snoring. Apparently, their night out had included plenty of alcohol.

David got out his flashlight and started reading his book again. After only a few minutes, the flashlight started to fade until it died out. David tried resuscitating it by giving it a few shakes, which brought it back to life for only a few seconds. "Cheap batteries," he muttered under his breath.

He pulled out the small wooden candleholders from under his bed, set them on his nightstand, and placed the half-melted candlesticks in them. David lit a match, touching it to both wicks, and watched as the flickering flames came alive. He lay on his back to get the angle of the light just right to illuminate the pages. Since it was late, he did not last long and only made it through nine pages before falling asleep. The book ended up on his chest and the candles leaked wax onto the nightstand as they burned through the late hours.

His dreams were random at first, touching on scenes from the book he was reading and playing on the emotions he had stirred up going through the boxes in the basement. After waking up and rolling around some, he drifted off again into a deep slumber. David found himself walking through a door into a darkened room. He heard a few tapping and ticking noises, but he could not figure out what was producing them. He continued forward. Tap. Tick! The noise was not following any particular rhythm, which made it annoying. Some of the sounds were more pronounced than others, and it occurred to him the noise was something hitting glass or plastic.

He opened another door and saw an old man hunched over a workbench illuminated by a candle. He held a small hammer in his hands. "Hello?" The old man stood up, much bigger than David had first thought. He raised the hammer as he quickly turned to face the teen. David threw up his arms to protect himself as he felt a searing pain in his right arm.

He awoke waving his arms, unintentionally knocking over the candles as he realized he was feeling the heat of the flame on his right forearm. David cried out in pain as he rolled off the bed. The candles went out after falling to the floor, spilling wax on the rug. He sat on the floor, cradling his arm and trying to calm down. Then, he heard another tick near his window. He crawled on his hands and knees towards the window, wondering what it could be. He slowly stood and opened the window, pressing his face against the screen and trying to get a look out into the darkness. Something small hit the facade of the house just below his window, spooking him back to his bedroom floor.

"Hey!" a voice called out from his backyard. David rose again and opened his screen, slowly sticking his head out. As his eyes adjusted, he saw the faint profile of someone standing under a tree. David pulled his head back in just enough that he could keep his eye on the figure while trying to stay out of sight himself.

Who the heck? he said to himself. The shadow stepped forward into the faint moonlight. It was that kid Luke from school! Why was that moron throwing stuff at his window? He stuck his head further out the window, asking in a hushed voice, "What do you want?"

"Come on outside. I want to take you somewhere," Luke answered.

"Are you crazy, kid? I'm not going anywhere. What're you doing here?"

Luke looked puzzled. "Didn't you read the note I dropped in your locker? I told you I was coming tonight around this time. Now get down here! I didn't ride all the way over here for nothing. We got something to do!" Luke's voice was growing louder with his increasing frustration.

So there had been a note. David considered the situation for a few seconds and knew he had to make a decision before his mom and Steve started stirring, let alone the neighbors. "First of all, keep your voice down before you wake up the entire neighborhood. I'll be down in a minute." He walked across his room and locked his door just in case his mother tried checking on him. He turned on the lamp and changed as he looked at his clock – 12:40 a.m. I can't believe I'm doing this, he thought. He turned off the lamp and opened the window screen all the way. He put one leg through the window and balanced himself with the other leg on the hardwood floor, bracing himself on the window frame.

As he ducked under the window he swung his leg out the window and touched both feet on the slanted roof. David used this same routine whenever he felt like sitting on the roof to get some fresh air or to sneak out for a late night ride. He gingerly tiptoed across the roof until he reached the chimney that rose up from the back of the house. He stepped down on the side of the chimney and gripped the edge of the roof as he inched his way over until his feet dangled off the brick chimney. He shimmied over until he could feel the deck railing with his feet. Once his feet were safely on the rail, he jumped onto the deck, landing as lightly as possible. As David stood from his crouch, he looked over at the tree, but did not see Luke. What the —?

Luke's voice startled David as he emerged from behind the tree. "About time. What were you doing, slowpoke?"

David ignored the comment and walked out into his back yard where their voices were further away from the house. "What are you doing here?" he asked in an aggravated tone.

"We're going for a ride." Luke grinned. David took a deep, annoyed breath and walked over to his bike.

He followed Luke as they cut through the neighbors' back yards, which led to a cross street. I can't believe I'm out with this kid, David thought as he pedaled along, looking at the houses that lined the block. Some houses had their front lights on while others were pitch black. He could hear wind chimes playing as they rode down the peacefully still street. "Where are we going?" David asked as they passed the library just outside his neighborhood.

"You'll see. I think you'll like it…no, you'll love it," Luke snickered as they veered off onto another road. They were traveling farther than David expected, not that he knew where they were going. On their next turn, they came to a dead end.

"Nice going, Luke."

"Take it easy, man. You could use a rest anyway. I was killing you up to this point."

"Whatever. I don't know why I even came."

"Hey, it'll be fine. Just have some fun, would ya?" Luke paused, "So what really happened with Brock down there in the woods?"

"I don't really want to discuss this right now."

Luke shrugged his shoulders. "Fine, have it your way. But you know you're not alone in this, right?"

The rest of the ride was quiet. Despite not wanting to talk, David felt a camaraderie with Luke knowing they both had been through the same thing with Brock. After a few minutes, they turned down another block, and Luke rode up the driveway of a random house, disappearing into the darkness. David slowed his bike by touching his feet to the ground, cautiously stopping in front of the house. He walked his bike up the incline and laid it down next to the parked car in the driveway. David quickly scurried along the side of the house over towards Luke as the teen crouched down beside a shed.

"Remind me never to bring you anywhere," Luke said sarcastically as David bumped into him.

"Shut up. What are we doing here?" David asked earnestly.

Luke sneered at David as he stood up and cracked his knuckles. "This is for all the other kids like us who have to deal with idiots like Brock." He bent down and grabbed a broken brick, weighing it in his hand. He looked at David. "Ready?"

"For what?" As the words left David's mouth, the broken brick was flying through the air toward the bay window at the back of the house.

CHAPTER 9

David froze as the glass shattered. Was this really happening? Luke sprinted for his bike and coasted down the driveway, making his getaway. In an instant, he had vanished into the night. David cowered behind the shed not knowing what to do, when a light went on in the house. Now panicked, he leaped up and made a break for his bike. He ran while pushing his bike to get some speed and hopped on.

"Call the frigging cops!" a voice boomed from inside the house. Pedaling away from the scene, David glanced back toward the house and caught sight of the mailbox that read 604 Shills. He looked up and saw the silhouette of someone looking out the second-story window. Brock?

He pedaled as fast as he could to make it under the dark cover of the tree-lined street. When he was about a half-block away, he heard a door slam and looked over his shoulder to see a man dart down the front lawn of the house and into the street wielding a baseball bat. "Get back here, you punk!" the man drunkenly shouted. He stumbled back up the driveway and yelled something incoherent at the house. When David hit the intersection, he turned left, forgetting which way they had come from. He heard the screech of tires as a car jerked into drive.

David was halfway down the next street and jumped a curb as he tried to stay out of the light of the streetlamps. He could hear the car's engine strain as it flew up the street parallel to the one he was on, then come to an abrupt halt at the four-way intersection. He knew he only had a few seconds until the driver decided which way to proceed. He hoped he had avoided being spotted and took the opportunity to pull up a driveway to wait for a few minutes. He could not take the chance of staying on the street and being seen, or worse, run down.

He quietly set his bike behind a bush at the top of the driveway, figuring he would be safe since no one would be up at this hour. He glanced at the darkened houses on either side of the shared driveway; it comforted him that the occupants were seemingly asleep. His concentration was broken by the heavy putter of the searching car off in the distance, and his nervousness grew. David knew he would have to improvise if he was to make it home safe, since he was not too familiar with this neighborhood. He would have to be smart about his every move to evade his pursuer.

After idling at the intersection, the car made a U-turn and drove back down the street. It was obvious that the driver had no clue where David was. After a couple minutes of catching his breath, David could hear the car approach again, this time coming from a different direction. He hugged the side of the brick house for a few seconds, desperately trying to stay still. Not feeling that he was out of view enough, he ducked into the back yard.

The car slowly made its way down the street as the driver examined the houses on either side. David then saw something he was not expecting – a flashlight shining up the driveway. His eyes grew wide with panic at the thought of his bike lying behind the bush. No, no, no, David pleaded to himself as the light floated back and forth. After a few long seconds the light drew back, and the car crawled on down the street. David then knew that if he were going to get out of this, he would have to do something very risky. He'd have to follow the car. If I can see him but he can't see me, that may give me a shot to escape, he thought. David knew he could not spend any more time sitting there. He had to get moving before the police got to the neighborhood. In his favor were the alleyways on this side of town, since he knew he could not stay on the streets.

After waiting another minute, David mustered the courage to mount his bike and head down the street tailing the car. It was almost at the end of the block. As the car puttered at the stop sign, David slowly pedaled his way towards the illuminated red brake lights. If he stayed on the sidewalk, the shadows of the trees would keep him out of sight. Then the right turn signal began blinking, baffling him. As the teen crept closer to the vehicle, it dawned on him he was making a mistake. Why would the man drive back toward his own house? David looked up to see the car start to make a quick U-turn at the intersection.

He had only made it about five houses from where he started when he had to quickly swerve up another driveway to avoid detection. He saw the flickering light of a television through a window as he stopped by the back door of the house. David knew he was in a bad spot but had no choice but to wait. The car drove a little faster down the block than it had before. Have I been spotted?

When the car passed, he readied himself to continue in the same direction he had first attempted, believing it to be the best way to evade the car. Suddenly, the kitchen light went on, and he heard the back door being unlocked. He took off down the driveway on his bike as he heard the door swing open. David whipped his head around to see an elderly woman in a nightgown with a broom in her hands.

"Intruder! Get out of here!" Down the street, the car screeched to a stop, then fishtailed wildly as the driver slammed on the gas and spun the wheel. David could hear the engine straining in pursuit as it grew closer by the second. He sped down the sidewalk and saw the entrance to an alleyway lit up under a streetlight on the next block. A police siren blared off in the distance. The cops are the least of my worries right now with this maniac after me, David thought as the car behind him blew through a stop sign. The driver had now caught up to the teen, driving parallel to him in the street. The parked cars were the only buffer between the two as David tried to maintain his velocity. With the entrance to the alleyway only a few feet away to his right, David hit the brakes, skidding his back tire to the left. He steadied himself, almost running into a stone wall that bordered the front lawn of the neighboring house, then turned into the alleyway.

The driver, not anticipating this move, slammed on the brakes and his tires smoked to a stop. He reversed the car, then jerked into drive and sped into the alleyway. Sparks flew from under the car as it bounced up and down on the uneven pavement. The worn asphalt slanted downward and dead-ended at a narrow cross street. The car slowed as the driver looked down both alleyways for the boy. He caught sight of the bike off to the right and throttled the engine. The car barreled down the alley, splashing through puddles that filled the pockmarked back street.

David was doing his best to avoid the holes as the car quickly gained on him. He turned with the alley as it bent sharply left, but could not see the large pothole camouflaged by pooled water. He splashed into the puddle while the impact of hitting the broken asphalt under the water jolted his feet off the pedals. He worked his way through the large, deep puddle and frantically started pumping his legs again.

Just behind him, the car flopped over the bumpy roadway as it negotiated the curve. The tires screeched trying to hold the turn, as it was sharper than the driver anticipated. The left front tire hit the cavity that had nearly taken David down and wobbled as it absorbed the shock. The driver lost hold of the steering wheel as the combination of curve and divot were too much for him to handle at once. The car swerved left, careening off the alley wall, and ricocheted back to the right. He desperately tried to regain control of the car but smashed into a pick-up truck parked under a carport, bending two of the support poles. The compromised structure creaked and then gave way, crashing down onto the hood of the car and shattering the windshield. The lights of the house came on, as did those of its neighbors, and loud, concerned voices emanated from the windows.

David stopped his bike and looked back at the destruction he had indirectly caused. A smile crept across his face. Someone would be facing drunk driving charges tonight. The car hissed and smoked as the driver struggled to open the door. He gingerly rolled out of the vehicle onto the ground, groaning. He spit out blood and closed his eyes, still in a daze. A remaining piece of the corrugated plastic carport roof slid off and shattered as it hit the cement.

David pushed off and rode into the darkness, trying to make do with the wobbly front tire of his bike. The wall that ran the length of the alley eventually met the ground and gave way to a small grassy hill. Now I know what the wild game felt like when my dad used to hunt, he thought. David rode up the hill to a stone path leading to an open field. Bumping along the path that intersected the youth sports fields, David saw his point of reference in the distance. St. Madeline's Elementary glowed under its outdoor lighting, and he knew exactly how to get home from here. David felt a huge sense of relief, but his thoughts now turned to the person responsible for this entire debacle – Luke. It looked as if the seemingly innocent kid had an agenda of his own. He would be avoiding him at school from now on.

He continued up the path and rode in back of the expansive schoolyard that led to another back street. David could now hear a second police siren, which was most likely headed to the alleyway. He rode past the school as fast as he could, trying to stay away from well-lit areas. The police sirens got quieter as David continued to distance himself from the chaos. Every few minutes he looked back to make sure no one was following him, but the rest of his ride home was uneventful.

He took a deep breath as he finally pulled up his driveway. He glanced around at his neighbors' houses to make sure no one was awake before he carefully put down his bike in the back yard and scaled his house. He eased his way back in the window, but lost his grip on the sill and tumbled onto the hardwood floor. David lay there motionless, just thankful that he was back home safe. He stayed on the floor for a minute, contemplating what had just taken place as well as listening to see if he had awakened his mother or Steve with his clumsy re-entry. When he was sure everything was quiet, he got undressed and tiptoed to the bathroom to wipe off the sweat and wash his face.

Back in bed, David knew he would have to stick around the house tomorrow. He did not know if anyone had seen him leaving Brock's house or the crash site, but he could take no chances. After the incident at The Shadows, he knew someone would point the finger at him for what had occurred tonight.

CHAPTER 10

The next day David did not wake up until almost noon. He walked over to his window and looked down at his bike. Dirt and leaves plastered it from the ride through the wet alleyway the night before. He grabbed a towel from the hallway closet and took a long hot shower to try to relax. He was still reeling from the events of a mere eleven hours ago, and he could not comprehend the complications that had come into his life in the past few days. Why did this happen to me? he pondered, but he already knew the answer: Brock. He was the cause of all this. David realized that if those boys had not picked on him down at the woods, this series of incidents never would have been set in motion. Those jerks are the reason Luke tracked me down at school and dragged me out on last night's insane bike ride.

Back in his room David dried off and dressed, still wondering how he would handle more unwanted attention. He didn't even want to think about seeing Brock, Sean and Joe. Running away would solve all his problems. But as distant as David was, he knew he could not leave his mother. She had already lost a son and a husband. Besides, running away would be like giving in to Steve somehow. Just as his mother did not want to give in to the town's skepticism and move after the accident, David felt the same way now. He refused to let Steve be the only male left in his mother's life.

David went downstairs to grab lunch since he had slept right through breakfast. His mom made him a salami and cheese sandwich as he took his place at the kitchen table.

"You really slept in today, David."

"Yeah, I was just really tired after this week."

"Well, I know what you have been through with school and all. You deserved a good night's rest." David allowed himself a small smirk, as his mother had no idea what had transpired the night before. After some more small talk with his mom, he finished up his lunch and headed outside. He had to see what damage his bike had sustained after the hellish ride through the alleyways. Just as he had suspected the night before, the front rim of his tire was bent. David grabbed an old towel from the garage, uncoiled the hose, and began spraying down his bike. It was not out of the ordinary for David to attend to his bike, so he knew it would not raise Beth's or Steve's suspicions. Getting all the mud and debris off his bike did not take very long. It was so fresh it had not had enough time to fully dry and paste on.

After wiping down the bike, he looked closely at the mangled rim. He needed to fix it today to avoid taking the bus this week. Depending on the day, Sean or Joe could be on the bus since their houses were on his route. Most of the time they would get a ride with Sean's older brother, Brad, but David knew the safest option was to repair his bike and avoid the bus. Since Brock's crew had started hassling him over the course of the past year, he tried to figure out ways to evade them at all costs.

David walked his bike over to the deck and balanced the handlebars on the bottom step. He attempted to hop on the tire to force it back in place, but after a couple minutes he knew this technique was not going to work. He groaned to himself. He would have to use Steve's tools. He knew Steve was in the basement, but he had no other choice if he wanted to fix his bike.

The teen walked down the basement steps slowly, then paused and bent down to see if Steve was asleep in his recliner. President Reagan was on the television discussing the USSR's recent nuclear testing. Steve was lying down and from this angle David could not tell if his stepfather was awake or napping. He had to get the tools regardless. As he crept down the stairs, David saw that Steve was not moving and then heard snoring. He walked across the basement to the closet that housed Steve's tools and quickly opened it. He flipped the switch that illuminated the cramped room and looked around to see what he could grab. He took the mallet that hung on the wall and then spotted a wrench he could use. As he reached for the wrench, it slipped and clanged against the cold hard concrete floor. David heard Steve snort and awaken from his Sunday nap.

"Beth, is that you?"

David calmly answered, "No, it's me, Steve. I'm just borrowing some stuff for my bike." He humbly picked up the wrench, feeling at Steve's mercy since he was using his tools. Steve sat up as David walked out from behind the door with the tools in his hands.

"What happened to your bike?"

His stepfather's interest in his project took David by surprise. He glanced down at the tools in his hands, trying to think of a quick lie. "Ah, nothing really. Came down hard on a tree root the other day and it bent the rim of my tire a little. Just trying to get it back in place."

"Need a hand fixing it?"

"Uh, nah, I should be okay, thanks."

Steve rubbed his eyes and watched as David crossed the room to walk up the stairs. "David, wait a minute. I know you and I haven't been on good terms lately and never really have been, for that matter. I'm hoping we can work on that. Your mother has had a tough time with your recent situation, and I just want to make things easier on her. I'm not saying you have to have deep conversations with me, but I think if we were more cordial toward each other, it would go a long way to easing your mother's mind."

David was not sure how sincere Steve was being, but he did care about his mother even if he did not always show it. He nodded. "Sure, I can do that."

Steve smiled and nodded to the TV saying, "We already have one Cold War going on, we don't need another one here."

David faked a grin and went upstairs thinking, You're still an idiot, but you're the least of my problems right now.

Back outside, David put the towel over the rim of the tire. He started lightly tapping the metal rim with the mallet until it became a rhythmic pounding, and the rim began to straighten out. After about a half-hour of forming the rim back into line and tightening up a few other parts with the wrench, his bike was about as back to normal as he could get it. If David had any trouble this week, the last thing he needed was his bike to impede his getaway.

In the house, David gingerly walked downstairs, hoping Steve was sleeping again. Once he reached the bottom of the steps, he heard Steve's muffled snores and saw a blanket draped over his face. The TV was replaying a news report of the failed Challenger space shuttle launch from earlier in the year. The television showed the infamous footage of the takeoff and subsequent explosion that he recalled all too well, having watched it live in school. David did not pay much attention in school except in his Current Events class, which piqued his interest because of the turbulent world events they discussed. David was drawn to tragedy. After all, he'd been through enough of it in his young life.

The news program played clips of President Reagan addressing the nation soon after the disaster. He still could remember how excited his dad had been about Reagan being elected five years ago. His father had felt that the new president was going to turn the country around, until Reagan was shot a few months after taking office. David found it ironic that his father thought the assassination attempt was a premonition of things to come for the country. It only turned out to be an omen for him – the boating accident occurred the following year.

The program moved on to the water salvage mission the U.S. Navy had undertaken to retrieve the Challenger crew compartment from the Atlantic. After the

56

rescue crew pulled the compartment from the ocean, they discovered the remains of all seven crewmembers still inside. This report transfixed David. He stared at the images as they flashed across the screen, while visions of his brother floating face up in the drainpipe flickered through his brain.

"Water, bodies, water, bodies," he whispered to himself.

Steve choked on his snore, breaking David's trance. The teen replaced the tools, making sure to be quiet this time so as not to endure another uncomfortable encounter with Steve. He slipped back upstairs unnoticed and went to his room to pull out the shoebox from the secret panel.

CHAPTER 11

Monday morning David went outside, grabbed his bike, and headed to school. The ride to school was peaceful, although he did flinch a few times when he heard the rev of an engine. Up until Brock, Sean, and Joe had started picking on him last year, he never really had a reason to be paranoid. Now he was always wondering. What if someone had seen him riding away from Brock's house? He pushed the thought to the back of his mind.

He pulled up to school, locked up his bike, and went through the motions of another day in the life of a high school student. People whispered to each other when they saw David as most of the school now knew about the rock incident down at The Shadows. David tried to stay vigilant, curious to see if anyone was talking about the broken window at the Shills house. All he could think about was avoiding Brock at all costs and making it through the day. He let out an audible sigh as he remembered the cause of this latest incident. Would that moron Luke tell anyone that he had smashed Brock's window? Or worse, would he tell them David had done it? I'm better off just keeping away from that kid, David thought. He made it through the first half of the day without seeing either Brock or Luke. He knew it would take a stroke of luck to not run into Brock before the end of the day, but he hoped for the best.

The second half of the day was as boring as the first, until David remembered that Sean was in his European Studies class. Last week Sean had made that scene right afterwards and got a talking to from Mr. Gavin. David couldn't imagine he would do something else. Sean gave David a shooting glance when he first walked in, but other than that did not pay much attention to him for the rest of the period. Mr. Gavin stood outside the classroom eyeballing Sean as he exited after class. David laughed to himself. He knew these guys would not be able to touch him in school unless they wanted to risk suspension.

David felt relieved at the end of the day to have not run into Brock or Luke. Just when he was feeling good, he turned the corner to see his nemesis standing at the opposite end of the hallway. David had completely forgotten that Brock's locker was down this hallway. He should have known to take the other way around school to avoid him. He backpedaled and peeked around the corner waiting for Brock to leave rather than take the long way to his own locker. A few kids gave David curious looks as they walked by, not knowing that he was trying to avoid his adversary. When David saw it was safe, he cautiously walked down the hallway. He turned the corner and glanced at his locker in the distance, hoping he could make it there unscathed.

"Hey, Collie!" a voice yelled through the bustle behind him. He froze, bracing himself for what was to come next. A hand landed on his shoulder, and David felt like everything was happening in slow motion. He did not have time to process whose voice it was and turned to face the person.

"Take it easy, Collie. Geez, I heard you were on edge, but calm down, man."

David slumped in relief. Evan, a kid he had known since grade school, stood in front of him with a grin on his face. While they were never close friends, they were far from enemies. Evan was in a couple of David's classes this year and, even though David made little effort talk to anyone anymore, Evan understood his attitude, knowing what he had been through.

"Hi, Evan." David tried to downplay his relief.

"Listen, David, I know the situation you're in with Brock. I'm not trying to get involved, but I just want to give you a heads up that I overheard Joe and Brock talking in Chemistry class earlier. It was definitely about you. Sounded like Brock was talking about something that happened over the weekend. Whatever it was and whether

59

or not you were involved, it sounds like you have a target on your back. Be careful around those guys."

Tell me something I don't already know. David said, "Thanks for the heads up, Evan."

The friendly teen quickly turned serious, grabbing David's arm and looking him in the eye. "Hey, there was something else – they said they would be looking for you after school." David rolled his eyes, then looked steadily back at Evan.

"Thanks for the warning."

"All right, man. No problem," Evan replied, clapping David on the shoulder and walking off.

After school, David paced back and forth by his locker wondering what route he would take home to avoid Brock. Because that idiot Luke had a score to settle, I have an even bigger bull's eye on me than before, he thought. The only way he figured he could make it home safely would be to ride around the back of the high school, across the soccer field, and over the footbridge. Even though that trek would take him completely out of his way and land him on the other side of town, it seemed the most secure.

He left his backpack in his locker, knowing he could not let anything slow him down. He took his time leaving school, but he knew that Brock could be staking out the bike rack waiting for him. By the time he mustered the courage to get moving, the only students left were the ones involved in after-school activities and sports.

David opened the door and peered outside, looking for any sign of the three bullies. A small group of students walked out through the door he was holding ajar, barely acknowledging his existence. David followed closely behind them, trying to blend in with the group until about halfway down the walkway. He darted across the lawn and kept moving towards the bike rack, making sure Brock was nowhere in sight. He quickly unlocked his chain and pedaled off towards the back of the school, nearly running over a few girls walking to the tennis courts as he turned the corner.

"Watch it, you weirdo! Go talk to yourself some more," one of them said as David rode down the incline to the grass athletic fields.

A few blocks from school, Brock and Sean sat in Brad Silver's black IROC-Z with heavy metal blaring, waiting for their victim. "Where is this turd?" Brad asked in a bored voice. "I wanna see an ass-kicking."

Brock looked out the window. "What time is it? He usually comes this way, and I couldn't be near school to do this. I think his house is in this direction," he said, pointing down the street.

"It's about four o'clock," answered Sean.

Brock appeared frustrated. "Give it a few more minutes, and then we'll ride around to find him. This dude is strange, so who knows what he's doing."

David rode through the fields as the soccer team was stretching for practice. He hesitated as he made it to the footbridge, which extended over a small creek and was a well-known spot for fights. He felt uneasy crossing the rattling wooden boards of the bridge, but once across, he breathed a heavy sigh of relief having made it this far without any sign of Brock. Maybe he's not after me today after all. Evan could have heard them wrong, he thought. David rode up the adjoining street with no sign of trouble, but he knew that he must stay attentive and not get complacent. He rode past a popular pizza shop where some kids were hanging out and angled his way back through the streets in the direction of his neighborhood.

Only a few blocks away, Brad Silver started up his car and drove down the block, trolling the streets for their victim. After a few minutes of driving around, Sean spotted a kid on a bike three blocks up. "Is that him?"

Brad stepped on the gas. "Let's check it out."

David thought better of riding in the streets and cut across a small park that was only a few blocks from his house. He jumped off the curb and was feeling much more confident since he was almost home. Brad coasted through two stop signs and reached the park David had just ridden through. He stopped the car as they looked around to see where the teen had gone.

"There he is," Brock said with a smirk, gesturing to the other side of the park. Just as Brad was about to step on the accelerator, a white car pulled out in front of them, then appeared to stall. Honking the horn, Brad stuck his head out the window.

"Get that piece of crap out of the way, man! What're you doing?" A hand waved in apology as the driver seem to signal that he had no control over what was happening. After about ten seconds, the car started back up and slowly pulled off. Sean watched the car pull away, taking notice of the peace sign on the bumper. Brad sped down the street, but no one knew which direction David had gone.

"I can't believe this!" Brock exclaimed, punching the dashboard.

Brad looked over, miffed at his passenger. "Easy on the car you meathead."

They drove aimlessly, hoping to catch sight of their prey, unaware that David was already riding up his driveway.

As David hopped off his bike, the white car that had just cut off his assailants slowly drove by his home. David opened the back door and glanced at the car, but thought nothing of it as he walked inside.

CHAPTER 12

At school over the course of the next two days, the news about Brock's vandalized house began to swirl. David treated it like the first go-round with the bully and chose to ignore the perception of his possible involvement. However, he worried that Brock's hostility toward him was growing, since they were now connected through two different incidents, both of which were to Brock's detriment. David assumed that Brock was biding his time and would take his chance for revenge soon enough.

The fact he had not run into his adversary earlier in the week surprised David. Even though he had spotted Brock from afar a few times, he did all he could to avoid a face-to-face confrontation. He figured he was lucky to make it home safe each day and was also glad not to run into Luke. He had never noticed him before last week, but David wanted to avoid that troublemaker as well. I hope Luke is avoiding me as much as I'm avoiding Brock, David thought.

By Wednesday, word had spread about the shattered window. Since almost everyone in school knew about the altercation down at the woods, they automatically thought there was a correlation between the two events. The student body was taking it upon itself to make assumptions about David and Brock since the rumors linked both their names. Some people in school had remarked that David was now walking with a little confidence and seemed more upbeat. At this point, David assumed no one positively knew he was present at Brock's house that night since no one had questioned or approached him.

Although he tried to downplay it on the outside, Brock's animosity towards David grew the more he heard the rumors. He could not lose everyone's respect when people regarded him as one of the most notorious kids in school. Brock prided himself on being feared, but was all too aware that his peers recognized David Collie as the source of all this upheaval. Ever since he had suffered the laceration and concussion down at The Shadows, he thought people were starting to view him differently. Word got around about David standing up to him, and as soon as that began to subside, Luke vandalized his house. This only led to more speculation about the two situations that shed a negative light on Brock. He knew he had let it go on too long, even if it had only been a week, and could only blame himself for not taking action. Something had to be done. Today.

David left his third-period class and casually walked through the flurry of the hallway between periods. He looked up at the 'Class of 1986' banner hanging over his head along with other décor that adorned the hallway honoring this year's graduating class. He failed to see Brock coming from the other direction, his target locked in his sights. As they drew within twenty feet of each other, Brock emerged from the crowd.

"Hey, Collie!" he shouted. "We gotta talk!" David swallowed hard and stopped in his tracks. The crowd quickly thinned out between the two. Brock looked around for any hall monitors as Sean and Joe materialized from the human sea to take their places by his side. Before David had time to react, Brock took a few strides toward him, pushing him up against the green lockers.

"Fight! Fight!" several bloodthirsty onlookers shouted as everyone had felt this moment building throughout the week.

Brock had David's shirt clenched in his fist so tightly that David was almost choking. "You like starting stuff, Collie?" With the distinct size advantage in favor of the aggressor, all David could do was struggle and squirm to get free. He dropped his books and tried to force Brock's grip off him but only looked helpless in his feeble attempt. "Guess what, Collie? I've been waitin' for this!"

The hold on David's shirt loosened, but a split-second later a punch into his midsection doubled him over.

Brock straightened him up against the locker and landed another punch to the left side of his face just below his eye. The power of the blow sent David crashing to the floor as the crowd gasped and then resumed cheering. David lay there, still, angry and embarrassed, with his eyes closed. He also felt a strange relief, as he had known this moment was coming and now it was over.

"Clear out of the way! Get out of here and go to class!" Mr. Gavin bellowed as he pushed his way through the cluster of students. "Holy mackerel," he said at the sight of the boy in a heap on the floor. David heard the uneven footsteps stop a few inches from his face as Mr. Gavin reprimanded Brock while he tried to help David up. "You like picking on people, Mr. Shills? Well, guess what? This one will most likely earn you a nice suspension!"

By this point, the other hall monitor, Mr. Crandley, had trotted up. "What happened here?"

"Get Mr. Shills here to the principal's office. I'm taking David to the nurse to make sure he's okay." David got to his feet with Mr. Gavin's aid as the bystanders began to disperse. "Looks like he got you pretty good, Mr. Collie. We'll need to put some ice on that eye to keep the swelling down, but you might develop a shiner. I tried to warn you after that last incident, son. You could've gotten help to stop this bullying." There was that word – son. David hated when people called him that.

So much for getting off easy with Brock. Now he found himself sitting in the nurse's office with a plastic bag of ice on his face. Mr. Gavin appeared in the doorway. "David, the secretary called your mother at work, and she's on her way to pick you up. Mr. Mitchell will be by to see you as well." David leaned his head back even farther over the back of the chair, dreading having to speak with his mom, no less the principal. After twenty minutes of sitting there with his eyes closed, trying not to think of the consequences of this latest episode, he heard his mother's voice in the hallway.

"Is he in here?"

"Yes, right this way," Mr. Mitchell said. Their footsteps echoed in the hall as they approached.

"Oh, my God!" Beth exclaimed at the sight of her son's face. She gave him a gentle hug. "Was it those boys again, David?"

David nodded in affirmation but protested, "It's not that bad, Mom, I swear."

His mother turned to the principal. "What, what kind of school are you running here? This is not the first time my boy has had problems with these kids. Where's the control around here? You'd like to think your child is in good hands and not have to worry about them when they go off to school."

Her comments disconcerted Mr. Mitchell. He waved the nurse out of the office and closed the door. "Ma'am, I realize that you are upset, and I understand your concerns. We try to ensure the safety of all our students and keep the peace among them as well. With that being said, we cannot be everywhere in the school at once. From what I understand, both our hall monitors were on the scene within a minute of the occurrence. These things happen in every school, Mrs. Mathis, but I assure you I will handle it."

David's mother, still upset, rubbed David's head and in a much calmer tone asked, "So where do we go from here?"

The principal paused and then looked at David. "Well, I know your son probably needs some time to rest up, so I would like to invite you to come in tomorrow so I can speak with you both in my office. Does 7:00 a.m. work for you?"

While still annoyed, Beth believed her point was made. "I would appreciate that, Mr. Mitchell. We'll see you tomorrow. Thank you." David stood up from the chair gingerly. He did not know what hurt more, his midsection or his face.

"Take care of yourself, David," the principal said as he opened the door for them. As they made their way down the hallway, a few passing students looked on and whispered to each other, snickering.

Roy Mitchell walked back to his office with Beth Mathis' harsh words still stinging. He sat down in his chair and quickly punched four numbers on his phone. The principal sank back in his chair with a slight grin on his face as he spoke. "Yeah, it's me. Listen, we just had another incident with David Collie. It's time to start the program with him. The time is right." He stood up. "I have them coming into my office tomorrow for a meeting to try and smooth things over. Once I get his mother alone, I'll discuss some options with her and bring you up to speed when the meeting is over."

Outside David and his mother put his bike in the trunk of the car. The ride home for David was a long one as Beth tried to hold back her emotions over her son's latest altercation. She did not understand how this could keep on happening.

"How can they be so cruel to you when you try to mind your own business?" She pressed him for details of how the incident had materialized. David tried to explain without going into specifics.

"Mom, it all happened so fast, I don't really recall everything."

Beth just shook her head. "Look at your eye, it's starting to swell up. We have to take care of that when we get home. Maybe we should make an appointment with the doctor if it gets any worse."

"Mom, enough. Please, I'll be okay. I just want to have time to myself." Beth took a deep breath, nodding her head in agreement, and wiping away a few tears that ran down her cheeks, streaking her makeup.

When they got home, David went upstairs to check the damage in the bathroom mirror. Looking at his reflection he saw that the area around his left eye was already puffy. I can't keep going through this. Something has to change. Back in his room, David lay on his bed thinking about how the next few weeks of school might play out. He also thought about the meeting tomorrow morning with his mother and the principal. What else could come of it besides discussing the obvious? There was a quick knock at his door as his mom opened it and silently handed him a bag of ice.

After lying on his bed for a while, he heard the back door shut, signaling Steve's arrival home from work. My mom is probably telling Steve all about this right now. Not that Steve cares, David thought. He pulled out the shoebox from his closet and opened the lid, peering inside. He sat in his chair by the window with the box on his lap and let his mind wander. He snapped out of his trance when he heard his mom call upstairs to announce dinner was ready.

Upon David's arrival in the kitchen, his stepfather greeted him. "How's the eye feel?" Beth shot him a look, but David did not seem to mind.

"Sore," David answered as he took his spot at the dinner table.

As they started eating, Steve turned to Beth, pointing with his fork in David's direction. "Do we have a steak we can put on that, Beth?"

David made an uncomfortable face, preferring to tend to his own wound. "I'll be fine, really. The nurse said I should ice it on and off for the rest of the night."

Steve shrugged his shoulders. "Okay, but there's nothing like a nice cold steak to help ward off a potential black eye." Beth let a smile cross her face. She was happy to see her two men getting along. Hearing them having a brief yet civil conversation allowed her some delight despite the circumstances.

Back in his room, David paid special attention to the icing intervals on his face, desperately hoping it would not get any worse. He could not keep his mind off what was to come the next day. Being the topic of conversation with the figurehead of the high school made him nervous. After tossing and turning, he decided to read to take his thoughts off the next day's meeting. A few pages in, he got to thinking about how a black eye would draw even more attention to him at school.

David snuck downstairs and grabbed a steak out of the fridge. He hoped it worked, although he would never give Steve the satisfaction of admitting it.

CHAPTER 13

The next morning David felt tired from only four hours of sleep, and the fatigue showed on his face when he looked in the mirror while brushing his teeth. The shadow of a black eye had developed, but he thought that the steak that now lay on the floor next to his bed had helped.

The drive to school was quiet as David and his mother were nervous, not knowing what to expect. As they pulled up to the building, David realized how strange it was to not see other kids because they were so early. The only people he saw were some teachers heading into school to get ready for the day. When he opened the car door to get out, Beth grabbed his hand. "Don't forget I'm going to pick you up after school."

He rolled his eyes. "Mom, I don't..."

"This is not up for debate. After what has happened lately, it's the best way to go."

They walked into the school and down the eerily quiet halls that would come alive in the next hour, jam-packed with students. David and his mother reached the office and were checking in with the secretary when Mr. Mitchell strolled in holding a cup of coffee.

"Good morning. Please step into my office." He nodded towards his door. A couple of girls who had principal aide duties glanced at David and his mother as they walked towards the office. The principal followed them, looking back at his assistant and giving her a wink as he closed the door. Everyone took their seats as the principal shuffled some papers on his desk and took another sip of coffee.

"Well, Mrs. Mathis, David, it is good to see you both. I wanted to be able to have this talk with you about the situation going on and my action plan. First, I want to apologize to you both, especially you, David, for what occurred. We do the best we can to protect our students from harm, but we can only do so much, and we expect our students to show respect for one another. I have taken swift action and imposed an out-of-school suspension on Brock Shills for five days. If we have another incident like this with him, I promise you an even harsher punishment will be laid down. Students attacking other students will not be tolerated. I want you both to know how seriously I take situations like this. I also take the utmost pride in offering a safe and comfortable environment for our kids to receive a sound education."

As the principal rambled on, David stared at him, trying his best to act like he was paying attention. He did notice that the man turned on the charm during conversation with his mother, although he was barely catching every other sentence because of his exhaustion. For over an hour Beth expressed her concerns and engaged the principal in problem-solving dialogue. She appeared content with how the conversation was going and it seemed that the discussion was drawing to a close.

"David, are you okay with everything we have talked about? I want you to know that I will do my best to see that this ends," the principal said.

Caught off guard, the teen stammered, "Um...ah, yeah. That all sounds good. I'm fine with that."

"Do you have any questions for me, son?"

David bristled. There was that word again. Didn't people think before they opened their mouths? He answered indifferently, "Nope, I think you covered it all."

"Good, good. I like to have a handle on what occurs inside these school walls. With all that being said, you are excused to join your first period class. Your schedule shows you're off to Ms. Wolff's geometry class. Thanks for coming in, David."

"Thank you, Mr. Mitchell," David said snidely as he stood up and gave his mom a quick smile. His mother reached for her pocketbook on the floor as he opened the door.

"Oh, Mrs. Mathis, would you mind staying a few more minutes if you can spare it?"

"Certainly, Mr. Mitchell," she replied. Beth turned to her son who stood in the doorway. "Have a good day, honey. I'll be by to pick you up after school."

The principal came around his desk as David turned with his mouth agape. Maybe this meeting was not as straightforward as it had seemed. "Thanks again, son," the man said as he shut the door. David stared blankly at this man he did not fully trust, and his anxiety grew as he imagined what he would be discussing with his mother. He walked down the hallway with his head down, feeling defeated, knowing there was nothing he could do.

Back in the office, Roy Mitchell was doing his best to make Beth feel at ease as he laid out his alternate plan to help David's situation. "Mrs. Mathis, as we have discussed here today, David has found himself in some bad circumstances of late, and I think I can help. As you know, your son likes to keep to himself and is not involved in school activities or the social aspect of high school, which is fine. Not everyone has to be associated with clubs or sports here at Jefferson High, but I am a little concerned with his well-being."

Beth looked surprised, not knowing how to take the last comment. "While I do appreciate your concern, I am his mother and would like to think I can take care of my own child."

Principal Mitchell took a breath and chose his words carefully since he felt he might have insulted her. "I know that you are a good mother because you are here today. You care about your son, and I do not doubt your parenting. At the same time, you cannot be here to take care of him at school, which is what I am here for. I wish nothing but the best for our students and strive to keep a positive atmosphere in these halls and classrooms." He paused. "I'll just ask you this flat out. What do you think of having David meet regularly with our guidance counselor?"

The question befuddled Beth. "Well, I want the best for David. Do you think something like that would help?" While she did not want to make any rash decisions, Beth knew she did not have many alternatives when it came to David's school life.

"This is a new program I want to start with kids who are having a tough time in school. We think we have some solid concepts to aid a young person who may be in an uncomfortable position, much like David is. A student's high school years can be the toughest in his or her life. There are a lot of changes, kids can be cruel, cliques are formed, and these years really can shape a young adult for the rest of their life. What they do now guides them on the path to their future. Our guidance counselor was a psychology major in college and has worked with helping teenagers at other schools." He paused. "Our counselor's name is Tyler Worthing. I can bring him down here if you would like to meet him."

Beth was quickly weighing her options, which were slim at this point. Her relationship with her son had been up and down ever since her husband and eldest son had passed. She knew that this might be the type of help David needed since things were so unstable in his life. She should jump at the opportunity. At the same time, she did not want to seem desperate. Beth thought, If I turn down this opportunity, would this man think I don't want the best for my own son?

She took a breath before answering. "Well, what you are saying sounds very comforting. The recent events have been very tough on him, and I obviously would like to see my son happier. So sure, I would be open to meeting your guidance counselor."

The principal nodded and picked up the phone.

CHAPTER 14

A knock at the door startled Beth. In walked a handsome, well-dressed man in his late twenties. The principal provided the introductions. "There he is! Mrs. Mathis, please meet Tyler Worthing." The young man extended his hand, smiling.

"It's nice to meet you, Mrs. Mathis. How are you?"

The man's charisma caused Beth to color slightly. "Nice to meet you, Mr. Worthing. I'm well, thanks." The guidance counselor sat down next to her in the chair recently vacated by David.

"Please, Mrs. Mathis, call me Tyler." Her blush reappeared.

Mr. Mitchell cleared his throat. "Well, let's get started. Tyler, Mrs. Mathis is David Collie's mother. David has run into a tough time lately with some other kids. Brock Shills, to be specific."

Tyler's brow furrowed. "Yes, I'm all too familiar with Mr. Shills."

The principal continued. "Aren't we all? I was just briefing Mrs. Mathis on our new program. She is interested in having David be one of the first to participate in this program, and I was hoping you could explain it in more detail since you are the man in charge."

Tyler shifted in his seat and adjusted his tie. "Well, sir, you are the mastermind behind it; I am just providing the expertise." The counselor turned to Beth. "This is a program that I believe will benefit kids who need a little encouragement to really come out of their shells, so to speak. Think of it as a personalized self-help seminar, just without the cheesy guru you always see on the infomercials."

Beth laughed a little as the counselor had her full attention. "I know what you mean, Tyler."

"What I propose is to set up regular meetings with the student, in this case your son. Maybe just a few times a week either before school, during classes, or after school. It's really whatever the pupil is most comfortable doing. Mr. Mitchell will allow him to leave class early or attend class late, depending on how he wants to do the timing of the session. We find it's better to talk with a student when they are most receptive. If you try to speak with a teenager who is filled with angst and not really in a good place, you will not get through. I know I probably don't have to explain that to you as a mother."

Beth seemed interested yet confused. "So, what will these meetings be all about?" she asked, leaning in closer to the guidance counselor.

"Well, I envision this as a talking session. Kind of like an interpersonal talk show, where we discuss what is going on in their lives and how they can help themselves. Maybe see what's bothering them or what they would like to change. I understand what David is going through. I was bullied as a kid myself, which is why I am here today trying to help students. I feel that if you get teens like David talking, it alleviates a lot of the stress they are feeling. Most kids in David's situation just want someone to talk to, but it has to be the right person."

Beth continued to listen intently to the counselor.

"My goal will be to help David see things in a different way. I hope to have him enjoy his high school experience more and perhaps get him more involved socially. I have worked at a couple of other schools and after teaching, counseling and researching, I think I have found a niche that has not been developed much. Sure, there are hundreds of guidance counselors in schools across the country, but they are not doing what we will be doing here. Other schools put a bandage on problems, but we are looking to make a permanent fix and make a positive change in students' lives. What do you say? Are you interested in having David participate?"

Beth pondered the proposal for a few seconds as she looked at the two men. "I'd be lying if I said I didn't think it was a good idea, but the thing is getting David to go along with it. I know that he tends to do things just to get me off his back, since I am somewhat of a nag." The two men let out a brief, forced laugh in order to comfort Beth.

After a few seconds of silence the principal spoke. "Mrs. Mathis, we can always give David some encouragement. If you speak to him at home and we talk to him here at school, maybe he'll be more apt to agree."

"Ok, I'll talk to him tonight. I'm sure he already knows something is coming, but please do not plan on meeting with him until you hear from me first. I'm not sure how this will go when I discuss it with him, but I will be in touch." The men looked at each other, trying to hide their grins, as Mr. Mitchell wrapped up the meeting.

"Mrs. Mathis, I really want to thank you for your time today. I promise this program will help David grow as a young man and will be kept strictly confidential. I will wait to hear from you before we proceed with anything. Here is my contact information."

Beth took the piece of paper, stood and shook each man's hand. "Gentleman, I want to thank you for your time and concern for my son. I will definitely be in contact. I'm a little nervous, but I'm hopeful about the progress my son will make with Tyler."

"The pleasure is all mine, Mrs. Mathis." The counselor turned to open the door and shot her a smile. Beth returned the smile as she left the office. The door closed as soon as she walked out, startling her a bit.

Am I making the right decision for David? she wondered as she walked towards the exit.

Behind the closed door of his office, the principal looked at the young man with satisfaction as he took his seat behind the desk. "So, Tyler, do you think we sold it to her?"

The guidance counselor felt a little apprehensive that they were not being completely forthright with what they had in mind for her son. "I think we did a good job. You and I both know she's desperate to help David. The tough part will be getting him in here. I've been studying his file and doing my own research. He doesn't seem like he will be the easiest person to sway. As much as he suffers in school, it's not because he's not smart, it's because he doesn't care."

Mitchell mulled over his coworker's words. "Yes, he's a tough one. But like any kid, maybe he'll go along with it to get out of class or to placate his mother. We'll soon find out."

Toward the end of the day, Beth Mathis sat at her desk contemplating how she should handle the situation. Tell David tonight or wait until the weekend? She did not want to stress her son out while he still had school. Friday night would be the best time to talk with him. She reached into her purse and took out the folded piece of paper with the principal's contact number. She dialed the phone and felt nervousness run through her body. She was still uneasy about this whole thing. "Yes. Mr. Mitchell, please. Tell him it's Beth Mathis. Thank you."

Roy Mitchell's deep voice came through the phone. "Hello, Mrs. Mathis. How can I help you?"

Beth's anxiety could be heard in her voice as she spoke. "About our talk this morning – I think I'd like to wait until tomorrow after school to speak with David. I just believe it will be easier to give him time to think about it over the weekend when he's away from school."

While the principal wanted to get down to business as soon as possible, he did not want to rush her. "I think that sounds like a good plan. If anyone knows a boy inside and out, it's his mother."

His response relieved Beth. "I'm glad you agree. Great. Well, I guess I will call you on Monday to let you know how it goes."

"You know what, when you talk to him after school tomorrow, just give me a call here if you get a chance. I usually work late on Fridays anyway."

Beth was a little surprised at his eagerness, but took it as general concern for one of his students. "No problem, Mr. Mitchell. I'll talk to you tomorrow night then."

The man sat back and wondered if he had come on too strong. "Screw it," he said aloud. "I've got this under control."

When David's mother came back to pick him up that afternoon, she did her best to act normal, knowing a big change would be coming for her son. Beth sensed that David knew something was afoot, but she had already made her decision to tell him Friday after school. Steve would be going out that night, and after David had time to relax she would talk to him.

Dinner that night was customary with Beth and Steve making small talk while David hurriedly consumed his meal. Just as he finished his dinner, his mother touched his hand. "I want to drive you and pick you up from school tomorrow."

David rolled his eyes. "But, Mom, I'm fine. Brock is suspended. You heard the principal yourself this morning."

She gave him a stern look. "David, as I said before, this is not up for debate. Just do me this favor, and I promise next week I'll leave it up to you if you want to take the bus or ride your bike. I wouldn't be able to live with myself if something else happened." David pulled his hand away and groaned.

The next morning on the ride in, Beth could sense her son's annoyance, but she knew driving him in was the right precaution to take. As David went about his day, he noticed that some people were going out of their way, more so than normal, to keep their distance from him. David knew he did not intimidate anybody at school, so he could not understand what was causing the apparent change. Usually most other students had little respect for him, but today some kids were actually getting out of his way to let David by in the hallway. What's going on here? he thought.

He did not come to the realization until later in the day during his history class when he saw one of the principal's aides whisper to a couple of other girls. They tried to play it off once they saw David looking at them, but right then he understood. He knew that she and the other aide had probably been gossiping about the meeting involving his mother. Maybe everyone is acting differently toward me because they think I'm untouchable. By now Brock's suspension was well known, and no one else wanted to risk drawing the ire of a hallway monitor or the principal himself. Maybe Luke saw this coming, which is why he avoided me as well, David pondered. The kid is smarter than I thought. He was grateful that the weekend was nearly upon him and that soon he would have a few days to relax and forget about all this stress at school.

A few miles away, Brock was laboring in his family's neglected and overgrown back yard. Since Brock was home during the day, his unemployed father put him to work to get his son out of the house. In addition to the yard work, his father handed the task of organizing the hoarded junk in their dilapidated shed.

The screen door swung open and smacked against the side of the house as Fred Shills stumbled through the doorway wearing a neck brace from the alleyway accident. He steadied himself on the railing with one hand while holding a bottle of whiskey in the other. He barked out incoherent orders to Brock who was sullenly raking up the debris that was strewn across the back yard.

"Yeah, yeah, I hear you," Brock replied, fuming.

"What you say, boy?"

Brock noticed how his father's drunken speech became a little clearer when his anger grew. He looked up at his father, and his eyes fell on the boarded-up bay window to the left of the door. Brock's rage intensified. I know Collie did this. That had to be him on the bike riding away. It's too much of a coincidence after what went on between us. That punch in the gut wasn't enough. He's got more coming to him.

"Boy!" His father's shout snapped him out of his daze. "Boy, pay attention. Get the hell up here and look at me when I'm talkin' to you!" Brock threw down the rake in frustration as he walked across the yard and up the steps, knowing what was coming next. His father looked at him with bloodshot eyes, his heavy breath reeking of alcohol. He did not say anything before giving his son a swift backhand across the face. Brock kept his head down as his father stumbled back inside. "That'll learn ya, boy."

Brock wiped his bloody lip. He was going to crush that Collie kid.

CHAPTER 15

After school on Friday, David headed upstairs just wanting to rest after another daunting week at school. He was eager to relax in the quiet of his own room and thought about going to The Shadows tomorrow for some time to himself. David knew he could tell his mom he was going anywhere else as long as she did not know he was going there.

He closed his door, figuring he would take an hour nap before dinner. After what seemed like only a few minutes, he heard his mom's footsteps coming up the stairs followed by a knock at the door.

"David?"

He knew there was no way he could ignore her. The fact that she had come to his room to speak to him most likely meant it was serious. Come to think of it, he had detected a bit of distress in his mother's demeanor on the ride home. The teen sat up as a thought popped into his mind. This is probably about the meeting at school. And how convenient, Steve's out tonight.

David opened the door without saying a word. His mother walked in and sat on the bed while David took the seat by the window and gazed outside. Beth knew she had to make this as quick and as delicate as possible.

"David, I wanted to talk to you about my meeting with the principal yesterday after you left his office. He presented me with a very interesting option that I think will be a positive step for you and I." His frozen gaze out the window broke a little, and Beth saw she now had his attention. "Mr. Mitchell introduced me to someone who laid out a proposal to address what's been going on with you both in and out of school. His name is Mr. Worthing, the guidance counselor."

David was vaguely familiar with Mr. Worthing, but did not know much about him except what he had overheard. He knew that some seniors met with him before graduating to discuss their future. He also knew that the guidance counselor had helped some other kids who had had deaths in the family or were struggling with school.

"During the meeting they explained that it could be beneficial for you to meet with Mr. Worthing, just to discuss what's been going on lately."

David looked his mother in the eye and bluntly said, "No."

Beth looked concerned but carried on with her attempt to sell her son on the concept. "David, before you dismiss the idea, just hear me out. I think..." David cut her off, his eyes boring into hers. "Mom, whatever it is, I told you, I'm not interested."

Beth's eyes began to fill up as she looked away, and David stared back out the window. There was silence for a minute as Beth regained her composure. "David, I'm not going to have you close me out like this again. Mr. Mitchell, Mr. Worthing and I just want to help you. You and I both know things have not been going your way, and it has to change. I can't just sit back and watch my son's life be turned upside down by some thugs. We have to make an effort. You have to make an effort. You can meet with Mr. Worthing to talk and figure some things out. I really don't..." David had heard enough and cut his mother off again with the same loud tone and stare.

"Mom, what don't you understand? I don't want to meet with anyone, I don't want to talk to anyone, and I don't want to figure anything out. I am who I am, and Mr. Worthing or whoever else is not gonna change that!"

Beth looked at her son intently. "I just want to be able to help you, and if you can't see that, then I give up." She got up and stalked out of the room, shutting the door with a force that showed David just how strongly she felt about it.

Later on David heard Steve come in after a night out. He heard their muffled voices through the floorboards and could tell by his mother's inflection that she was still upset and had probably been drinking. David could hear her talk about the plan to help him at school and his objection to it. There was a sudden thud in the kitchen, followed by "Unbelievable!" David presumed Steve had hit the counter with his fist, showing his frustration with his stepson.

David smirked as he found Steve's disingenuous outburst comical. Nice show, Steve, you loser. Maybe my mom buys your act, but I sure don't. I can't believe my mom thinks you really care. As he lay there in bed, David knew he was being difficult with this whole school counselor ordeal. Part of him did not want to hurt his mother's feelings, but he also did not want anyone to interrogate or study him.

After some quieter conversation in the kitchen, he heard his mother walk upstairs while Steve went to the basement. The sounds of the night's hockey game playing on the television drifted up through the vent. How does my mom not see what a jerk this guy is? David took a deep breath and tried not to think about his trouble at school or the rekindled unstable atmosphere at home. He delved into a book to try to lose himself in a fictional realm and forget about the current state of his real world.

He read for a while, then started to think about the conversation his mother had tried to have with him earlier. One person he knew might be able to help him talk things through was his friend Aaron. The teen looked down at the phone on the floor, paused for a moment, and then picked it up, quickly dialing. He explained the situation to Aaron and listened to his friend's response.

Within a few minutes David started to consider some crafty reasoning from his friend as to why he should take up the offer to meet with Mr. Worthing. Appeasing his mother and the principal seemed like two good reasons. If David went along with what seemed like an innocuous counseling session, maybe it would divert some of their attention elsewhere.

83

"Besides, dude, you can just fake it. That or stall if you do not feel like talkin'. They can't force anything on you."

"Thanks for straightening me out, man."

"No problem."

"Okay, Aaron, I'll meet up with you sometime soon."

The next morning David woke up early. He left the house before his mother or Steve were up, as he was eager to ride his bike and clear his head. Talking to Aaron had really opened his mind, and he was not as intent on just dismissing the whole idea of talking to Mr. Worthing.

As he rode aimlessly around the neighborhood, he thought about last Saturday's incident and the destruction Brock's father had caused with his car. I wonder how that alley scene looks now, he thought. He made his way across town and found the alleyway that had been a living nightmare only a week ago. David traced that fateful ride, getting a daytime look at the narrow road and its potholes that had caused him so much trouble that night. He approached the carport and saw that it was almost completely deconstructed. Only two poles remained upright, and there still was some broken glass on the ground.

David knew he could not stop and stare at the wreckage since he did not want to draw attention to himself. He rode past it slowly, grinning at the thought of that dumb drunk ending the maniacal chase by smashing into someone's property. As he rode on, David saw a coach conducting tee ball practice on one of the athletic fields to his left that bordered the alleyway. I wonder if any of those kids will have to go through the same thing I have in their lives, he pondered.

David pedaled out of the alleyway and turned onto the connecting street. He made a turn at the end of the street and continued to enjoy his ride for a couple blocks, not even thinking about the area he was in.

He glanced to his right and in disbelief realized that he was looking at Brock's house. Not being too familiar with the area, he had inadvertently ridden right in front of number 604. David pedaled quickly down the street, trying to get out of the vicinity as soon as possible.

At that moment, Brock came down his driveway with the lawnmower, his eyes locking on the fast-moving bicyclist. As he stared at the kid on the bike, a look of shock crossed his face. I knew David Collie was behind smashing my window. That kid has a lot of nerve coming back here. He'll definitely get his when I get my shot.

David sped down to the woods and rode across the rocky terrain that led to his home away from home. He disappeared into the woods in the direction of the pipe where he had left the note for Patrick. He wondered if Patrick would be there today, and if he had gotten his note. He had to hop off his bike once he got in deep, as the roots and stones of the uneven forest floor made it difficult for bike travel.

After a ten-minute excursion, he made it to the pipe and laid down his bike. He walked along the metallic cylinder and saw that while his makeshift paperweight was there, his note to Patrick was not. David felt a small sense of relief that his friend had gotten his letter. Hopefully, he would understand.

He looked around for a few minutes to take in the scene, and then looked up at the train bridge, thinking it seemed like a good place to relax. David walked his bike over to the base of the hill and left it leaning against a tree. He scaled the steep incline, slipping in the loose dirt, and made his way to the top, then walked along the section of the tracks that spanned the river. He sat down in the middle of the bridge and just looked down at the water for a while. He contemplated how years ago this same body of water had taken his father and brother. He thought about how things would be different if they were still alive.

What if I had gone along? Would this still have happened? Could I have done something to help? What would Sam's life be like if I was the one who died? He leaned over farther and stared into the dark water of the cruel river that had swallowed half his family. If I decided to jump and changed my mind when I hit the water, I wouldn't be able to make it.

His mind wandered back to the discussion with his mom and what Aaron had told him on the phone. What if I did go along with this guidance counselor meeting? I could just fake it through a handful of meetings until they believed I was better like Aaron suggested, I guess. Meanwhile, I could get excused from a couple of classes and maybe even leave school early.

When he actually considered it, it didn't seem that bad. David knew there was nothing to lose and that he had to improve some aspects of his life in order to go back to what he deemed his own normalcy. It was apparent that he would just have to go home, apologize to his mom, and tell her that he would give it a try. He had no intention of actually getting too involved in these sessions with Mr. Worthing though. He had heard that the counselor was very passionate about his students and never gave up on a pupil no matter the case. It seemed to some people that he had a self-righteous obsession with trying to make an impact on the lives of kids he felt needed it. That guy isn't going to get too far with me, but I'll manage with his nonsense.

David reclined and rested his elbows on the railroad ties. He knew he would have to get up soon since a train was probably due. He peered out over the treetops of The Shadows and smiled at his paradise. He really did enjoy this place and knew that it would always be here for him when people were not.

As he looked over the horizon, he noticed smoke rising up from a section of the woods he did not pass through very often, even though it was not too far away. That's strange, he thought. Either someone is starting a fire or a brushfire has sparked up. I'll have to check it out.

A moment later he felt a slight vibration, but the smoke still held his attention. He started to walk down the tracks and felt the vibrations turn into a rumble. Was the train that close? He thought he had more time. David was not one to panic, and this situation would be no different. As he reached the end of the bridge, he could see the train in the distance. He stood there on the tracks, staring at it as What if? crossed his mind. The horn sounding broke his daze, and he hopped off the tracks with the locomotive only about one hundred feet away. He slid down the steep incline, taking some small rocks with him. Mid-descent David took another quick look at the smoke that emerged from the treetops and got a good sense of the area it was coming from. He regained his balance at the foot of the slope and looked up at the passing train, then grabbed his bike and walked back into The Shadows in the direction of the smoke.

CHAPTER 16

David maneuvered his bike over the lumpy terrain. Looking around, he knew he was heading into an area of The Shadows he did not normally frequent and needed an escape plan just in case. David could see the smoke through the trees and decided it would be best to continue on without his bike. He shoved it into a thick bush so that it was fairly hidden and walked on towards the fire. The river was about a hundred feet off to his right. David knew if he were to get in trouble, he could run back to his bike and ride along the riverbank against the perimeter of the woods.

As he approached the suspected area, David squatted down to inspect the scene and saw the unattended fire. Maybe this person or people had moved on and left it to burn out. After a minute, David figured it was safe to approach the fire. He cared deeply about these woods, and he did not want to risk a brush fire starting. Whoever had built the fire apparently knew what they were doing. They had formed a ring of rocks around the carefully placed pieces of timber, just as David's father had shown him on a hunting trip when he was young. He began kicking dirt on the flames when he was startled by a voice.

"Hey, kid, what the hell you doing?"

David froze as he heard footsteps come closer. He turned to see a haggard man in his early fifties with an annoyed look on his face. It appeared the man had not showered in quite some time and his clothes were too big for him, hanging off his wiry body. A thought came to David as he stared at the man who stopped about ten feet away. It had to be the person who set up the campsite he had seen last weekend. The vagrant was holding a fishing pole and tackle box in one hand and a freshly caught catfish still on the hook in the other. "I was about to cook this on that fire you're trying to extinguish."

David stammered as he grasped for words, and mustered a weak "Sorry." The man squinted as he looked David over.

"You know, I've seen you here before, boy. Down in these woods." The petrified teen swallowed hard. He did not know what this man was capable of or if he was some kind of lunatic. His legs tensed as he prepared to flee. "You're that kid who's always down here running around, playing all over. I've seen you quite a few times. You know, you're a strange one."

I'm the strange one? A bum who was apparently living in The Shadows thought David was abnormal? He was sure the homeless man was going to mention seeing him rummaging around his makeshift campsite last week. But David remembered the head that had ducked behind a bush – that person's hair was clean and short. This weirdo had long, messy hair. It couldn't have been him.

The way this vagrant was talking seemed more friendly than threatening. This guy is kind of like me. An outcast, David thought. Feeling more at ease, he decided being cordial was the best way to handle the situation. "Uh, yeah, I do come down here often. It's kind of like a place to get away. I'm usually hanging out with my friend."

The disheveled man's eyes widened a little as he nodded his head. "Right. Now that you mention it and I hear your voice up close, I think I've heard you yelling at someone. Probably your friend, like you said." The homeless man walked around David, sat down on a large rock by the fire, and pulled a knife from his tackle box. David took a step back. The man looked up at him with a laugh. "Relax, would you? Now you're making me nervous. Take a seat. I'm just going to fillet my meal. What's your name, son?"

David sat down on a stump and looked into the fire as the man threw on a few more sticks. There it was again, that word – son. "It's David. My name is David," he said in an annoyed tone.

The man sat back as he steadied his catch on a rock. "You know, I saw that incident you were involved in the other week." He motioned with his head in the direction of the old water treatment plant. "I was there when that boy was hit with the rock."

David rolled his eyes at the thought of having to go through this explanation again. "Well, I didn't do that. It was my friend Patrick, the one I'm usually down here with. Besides, that jerk had it coming."

The homeless man began sawing off the head of the fish. "I never said you did anything wrong. I had a good view and knew what they were doing. Like I said, I've seen you down here often since I took up shelter in these woods. Why are you always down here? Why aren't you out playing baseball or doing other things kids do?"

The conversation was starting to irritate David. "What's with all the questions? What's your name anyway?"

The man laughed at the boy's defensive demeanor and carried on filleting his fish. He answered in a calm tone. "I didn't mean to get under your skin, David. I was just curious. I know you probably have been coming down here longer than I have. Sorry if I offended you. I didn't intend to. The name is Eugene. I've been lying low down here for a few months now. I'm originally from out west a little ways."

David studied Eugene's surgical technique as he cleaned the fish. "Well, what brought you down to these woods?" Eugene put down the knife and placed the fish on a rock in the middle of the flames.

"I actually have been traveling for quite some time. I was in the Vietnam War in the early 70s, and when I came back I just didn't feel right. I was still living with my mother. My father left us when I was little, so he was never really in the picture. After being home for a while, I had some problems coping. My mother and I started arguing more and more. Maybe it was her. Maybe it was me.

Maybe it was both of us, I don't know. Well, things only seemed to get worse from there, and I started drinking a lot. One day everything just boiled over and I left."

David squinted thoughtfully. The man's story intrigued him. "What happened? What did she have enough of?" Eugene grabbed a stick and stoked the fire, causing ashes to float up into the air.

"Uh, that was a tough time. I made some bad decisions." He wiped his brow and hesitated. "You really want to know?" David nodded, listening closely.

"Well, I was out of work, just pretty much drinkin' my days away, along with getting into some other things. My mother would get on me every so often to pick myself up and get a job. Kept nagging me to get out more often, you know, stuff like that. Well, one day I was in my room upstairs listening to music, working on a bottle of Jack or something, I'm sure. She opened my door and started in on me when I was half drunk and in a sour mood. I got up and we screamed in each other's faces.

"While we both were stubborn, whenever we would argue she was always the bigger person and would walk away first. But I wasn't finished with my say when my mother walked out the door. I followed her into the hallway and grabbed her arm. She pulled away from me and started for the stairs. Being half-drunk, I stumbled after her and bumped her pretty hard, which sent her down the stairs. The noise of her body tumbling down the steps and hitting the landing at the bottom made me sick to my stomach. I just stood there as she lay motionless at the bottom of the steps. I didn't know what to do except leave. I grabbed all the necessities that I could fit in my duffel bag."

David had to turn away for a moment. He had not expected this man's story to be so emotionally charged.

"When I walked past her body, I could see that she was still breathing and that she had a broken leg and a cut on her forehead. I knew it would be very hard for her to

---

91

ever forgive me, even though it was not purposeful, let alone let me live in the house. I called an ambulance and left her a note. I was long gone by the time they got there.

A few weeks later when I had already traveled a couple hundred miles east, I called her from a pay phone. When she answered, I couldn't even speak and just hung up, but I think she knew it was me." Eugene cleaned off his knife on some leaves and used it to shift the fish around on the rock.

David took a deep breath. "Wow, that's heavy. And I thought my relationship with my mom was screwy." They sat there quietly for a few minutes. Going along with this counseling plan of his mother's didn't seem so bad compared to what Eugene had just shared. Even though they had just met, David felt a bond with this man. Here was someone who could understand him.

Eugene finished cooking his fish and grabbed a plate from his bag. "Well, David, sorry to dump all that on you, but I'm a bit of an open book. You seem like a good kid. Any time you're down here and wanna talk or hang out, just let me know. I'm right over there." Eugene gestured over his shoulder, and David saw the blue tarp he had stumbled across last week. "Now you can put out that fire, kid. Then would you mind helping me carry some of my stuff back to my setup over there?"

David resumed kicking dirt on the fire. "Sure, sure, no problem." Eugene started off in the direction of the blue tarp with his freshly cooked fish and tackle box. David grabbed the rest of Eugene's things and followed the man back to his campsite. As he approached the tent, Eugene turned suddenly.

"Stop!" David froze in his tracks, eyes wide. He trembled as he stood there, fearing what was coming next. Eugene walked over to the frightened boy, knife in hand. David wished he had just run instead of standing there, feeling all too vulnerable. The vagrant bent down on one knee in front of David and swished his knife around in the leaves until they heard the clink of metal on metal.

"Ah, there it is," Eugene said. He twisted his knife, disarming a contraption hidden in the ground. "Walk around that way and over that log," he instructed David as he gestured with his hand. After the teen calmed down, he made his way along Eugene's suggested path.

"What the heck was that?"

Eugene itched his bushy beard with the knife. "That, my friend, is a trap. I have to protect my place somehow. There are a few of them around. Just sit down on the log, don't move, and you'll be fine." David's eyes grew wide again as he thought about how close he had probably come to hitting a trap when he first stumbled upon this campsite.

Eugene moved around some belongings under the tent and sat on his sleeping bag. "Sorry about that. I think someone may have been rummaging around in my stuff lately. But seeing you down here now, I wouldn't want anyone to get too hurt. My stuff isn't worth it."

The teen flashed back to the day when he first saw this setup and wondered, Who could have been following me that day if it wasn't Eugene? I'm better off keeping that story to myself. If that other person took something, Eugene might blame me. David was now on edge, so he quickly changed the subject. "No problem. Thanks for the heads up. How long are you planning on staying here?"

Eugene scratched his head and looked around at his things. "Ah, I don't know. Haven't really thought about it much to be honest with you. I guess when the time is right, I'll move on. I usually know when it's time to relocate. Just an inkling I get, ya know? Unless something occurs that forces me out first." The two talked a while longer about The Shadows and shared some more stories until David broke off the conversation.

"I have to head back to my house before my mom starts to worry about me."

———

93

Eugene stood up. "I'll walk with you. My legs need a stretch. Does your mom always worry about you?" David let him lead the way out of his booby-trapped campsite, waiting to answer so he could concentrate on his own footsteps.

"I guess you could say she's a worrier. After you told me about what happened with you and your mother, I got to thinking about mine. We had an argument yesterday, and she's probably wondering where I am since I left the house early this morning without telling her." The homeless man raised his eyebrows. David thought for a moment about how he wanted to phrase things as they walked towards his bike. "My mom and I have weird kind of relationship. She was always on my case when I was younger, but has been a little freer with me as I've gotten older. We're not as close as we once were since she remarried. I just kind of keep to myself, but try not to totally ignore her. But she is my mom, and I know I can only push her away so much."

Eugene nodded. "Do you still speak with your father even though your parents aren't together anymore?" They reached the bush that hid David's bike and he pulled it out.

"Ah, he's not around anymore. I haven't seen him in quite a few years." David barely discussed the accident with people he knew, let alone someone he'd just met. He quickly changed the subject back to his mother. "The disagreement with my mom was about something at school. They want me to meet with a counselor since I've been getting bullied, but I'm not sure if it's for me. I have been reconsidering it today though." Since Eugene already knew about the bullying David was prone to, having seen it firsthand, the teenager had no problem opening up about the latest run-in with Brock at school.

After listening to the story, Eugene shook his head and let out a sigh. "You know what, I can relate to you, David. As a young boy I used to get picked on myself. I

———

94

was shorter than most kids, so the insecure tough guys took advantage of that. I always wanted to get back at the kids who pushed me around."

David smirked, thinking, So would I.

"Why do you think this Brock kid and his buddies continue to get on you?"

David shrugged his shoulders. "I don't really know. I guess I'm different. It seems like the more I try to keep to myself, the more things happen to me. I think that's why my mom and the principal want me to speak with this guidance counselor guy." They walked on quietly for a few minutes as David guided his bike along the lumpy dirt path, then Eugene spoke up.

"Well, David, I'm going to head back. Do your mom a favor and talk to her when you get home. If she really wants you to speak with someone at school, what harm could it do? You could just go through the motions at each meeting. It's not going to last forever."

"Yeah, you might be right."

"If he thinks you are getting better, I'm sure they will end the sessions. As far as that kid who keeps picking on you, just stay away from him. Try to avoid any place in town you think he might go, steer clear of him in the hallways, and don't even make eye contact. From what you've told me and what I saw down here that one day, it sounds like something is a little off there."

"I appreciate the advice, Eugene. Maybe I'll stop by to see you next time I'm down here."

Eugene patted him on the back. "Sure thing, David. I'll be here. Take it easy. And learn your lesson from me – give your mom more respect. Things probably aren't easy on her either when you're going through tough times. I'll see you later."

David smiled and walked his bike toward the gap in the shrubbery that led to the street. He turned to say something else, but Eugene had already disappeared into the thick brush.

Before he headed home David rode around for a short while thinking about how he should approach his mother about meeting with the guidance counselor. After talking to Aaron on the phone last night and Eugene today, he realized that it was probably in his best interests to move forward with the sessions. If talking to someone helped him avoid a situation like Eugene's, it was worth it.

CHAPTER 17

David pedaled faster, figuring his mother was likely worried about him, not knowing where he had gotten off to this morning. It started to drizzle as he rode through his neighborhood on his way home, but he did not mind since it soothed him a bit. Rain seemed to fit the teen's melancholy personality. Despite his present open-mindedness, David knew that the counseling sessions would not change him much, as he was not easily swayed and content with the way he currently lived his life, aside from the added attention. As he rode up his driveway, his stomach sank a little at the thought of the awkward greeting that awaited him. Will she yell at me? Will she cry, thinking I ran away from home? He wheeled his bike into the garage, then stood in the driveway and stared up at the sky as storm clouds hastened the arrival of twilight. A few raindrops hit him in the eyes, blurring his vision.

He walked to the door rubbing his eyes and could see his mother doing dishes. As he turned the knob she looked out at him and her eyes grew wide with surprise. That in itself confirmed what he already had predicted; his mom thought he had run away from home. Because he had left before she was up this morning, for all she knew he could have snuck out in the middle of the night. Just play it casual, David told himself. "Hi, Mom," he said as he walked in the door.

Beth stood there with eyes wide and mouth agape. Her voiced cracked slightly as she spoke in a slow, firm tone. "You had me worried sick. David, where have you been?"

Before he could answer, she strode forward and wrapped him in her arms. He did not answer immediately as his mother sniffled in an attempt to hold back her emotions. After a few long seconds she let him go and held his shoulders, looking him in the eye. "Don't ever leave this house without telling me first, David. Being a mother, I always fear the worst. Especially after what this family has been through."

He scratched his head and spoke cautiously. "Sorry, Mom. After our talk last night, I just needed some time to think. I just went for a ride. I should have woken you or at least left a note."

Beth looked at her son with disapproval of his answer, but knew he would not give her much more. "Well, David, since you had the entire day alone, what were you thinking about?"

Knowing that he probably just put his mom through some of the most stressful hours she'd had in a long time, he spoke carefully. "Well, Mom, I had time to think about what I have been through lately, and I think these meetings with Mr. Worthing are for the best. I also know this is what you want for me."

Since he was a kid of few words, his mom appreciated his response. She smiled and gave him another hug while whispering in his ear, "David, I know this will improve things. I would not put you in any situation that I did not think would put you in a better position in life."

David nodded. "I know." She gave him a kiss on the forehead, and David headed upstairs. I guess I'm committed now.

The next day when David awoke, he found that his mother was out running errands and Steve was cleaning out the garage. He took the opportunity to sneak down to the basement. He pulled the string to turn on the light of the back room and began sifting through boxes of his father's and brother's keepsakes. After a few minutes, he came to the heavy foot locker with the contents he was looking for. He grabbed a few items out of the locker, put everything else back in place, and hurried upstairs. In his room, David hid the items in the back of the closet, covering them with some clothes and an old blanket, knowing his mom would not be too happy to find them in his room. The rest of the day he laid low as another storm blew into the area, bringing Steve back inside as well as his mother home from her abbreviated errand run.

Monday morning, David's mother drove him to school, but agreed to put his bike in the trunk so he could take a ride after school. Beth figured most of the reason why her son was doing the sessions was to appease her, yet she hoped that he was at least a little invested in making a change. After locking his bike at the rack, they went inside only to find that Principal Mitchell was not available. His secretary had the permission form and other paperwork ready for Beth to sign in the administrative office.

Mr. Worthing came down to greet them while Beth was finishing with the papers. "How are you, Mrs. Mathis?" he said, shaking Beth's hand lightly.

"Hello, Tyler. Very well, thank you."

The guidance counselor turned to David. "Your eye is looking better, David." The teen mumbled a "thank you," hoping to close that topic. Beth handed the paperwork back to the secretary, and Mr. Worthing offered to take them down to his office so she could see where the counseling would take place.

The first thing David noticed was that the guidance counselor had to unlock his door. This guy had to only be gone for a couple minutes and he locks his door? he thought. David noted that everything was very neatly placed on the shelves, desk and walls. On the desk there sat a small analog clock situated between a mini globe and a Rolodex. A Rubik's cube, already solved, sat atop a few stacked files. The filing cabinet in the corner had alphabetized labels on the front of each of the five drawers. A painting of a countryside hung on the wall behind the desk.

"Well, this is it," the counselor said, arms extended.

"David," Beth said, jarring her son out of his daze. "What do you think? Seems nice to me."

David looked over the other objects hanging on the wall – a boring painting of a meadow with a small bridge spanning a narrow creek and the counselor's college diploma. "Not bad."

"It's comfy," Mrs. Mathis noted as she looked at Mr. Worthing with a smile. "Well, David, I'm fine with everything if you're comfortable." David just nodded.

"I want to thank you for coming in again, Mrs. Mathis. I really think this will be a good step forward. I'll discuss David's schedule with his teachers and try to get our first meeting set up this afternoon if that's okay."

Beth again looked over at her son. "David, if you are ready today and want to get started, I think the sooner the better."

David shrugged his shoulders. "Yeah, that's fine with me."

Mr. Worthing smiled at the small progress he seemed to be making with his subject already. "Ok, Mr. Mitchell and I were looking at your second class after lunch. Your schedule says that would be your art class." The counselor looked at David, who did not give any noticeable response.

Mrs. Mathis spoke for her son. "Yes, Tyler, that's fine. Not that I'm not an art person, but I would rather he miss electives than core classes."

Mr. Worthing put the schedule on his desk. "Well, I guess that's all we need right now. I'll see David later on today, and again, I appreciate you coming in today, Mrs. Mathis." He smiled warmly at her. Beth gave David a hug before they went in opposite directions. David walked down the hall and his mother turned to get one more glimpse of her son before he rounded the corner.

David's trepidation increased throughout the day as his appointment with Mr. Worthing drew closer. He started second-guessing his decision to go along with the plan even if it was just to gratify his mother. He became preoccupied with trying to think of the questions that the counselor may ask and topics they would cover. How do they even expect this to help me? he wondered as he stared out the window.

"Mr. Collie, are you paying attention?" his algebra teacher asked, snapping him out of his thoughts. "What is the answer to the problem I have on the board?"

David flipped through his homework book fruitlessly looking for the answer. "Uh, I couldn't figure that one out." A few kids chuckled at David's flat response.

The teacher peered over his glasses at David with a dissatisfied look, his mustache scrunched up touching the tip of his nose. "That's minus points, Mr. Collie," he said, making a note in his binder. "Perhaps you should spend more time staring at your algebra book than out the window."

When the time came for David to meet the counselor, he thought about skipping the meeting altogether and just going to art class. However, he knew it wouldn't work. The teen knew there was no way out of it since he had already agreed to it and his mom had signed off.

David stopped at his locker to put his books away before heading to Mr. Worthing's office. He spent a little more time at his locker than he normally would, feeling nervous. When the bell rang the hallway cleared, leaving David by himself. He spent a few minutes reorganizing his locker, trying to delay the inevitable. He grew increasingly resistant to the thought of the meeting as each second passed, trying to think of anything he could say or do to get out of it. When David heard the click of dress shoes coming down the hall, he shut his locker and turned to see Mr. Worthing approaching with a smile on his face.

"David, there you are. I was just going to your next class. I thought you might have forgotten."

David looked up nervously at the counselor. "Ah, no, no. I just had to clean up my locker. I opened it and some of my books fell out. I was coming down right after this."

Mr. Worthing shook his head with a laugh. "Well, I'd be lying if I said that hadn't happened to me before too back in my school days." David looked at him blankly, not responding to the quip. "All ready to go?" the counselor asked with a double knock on the neighboring locker.

"Yeah, sure." David thought, What's this guy's rush anyway? What am I, two minutes late? As they walked into the office, David noticed that Mr. Worthing had swapped one of the straight-backed chairs with a lounge chair. During his last visit, the counselor had the recliner pushed against the far wall holding stacks of files. Don't tell me this guy is going to have me lie on that thing.

"Give me a minute here, David, to get some things together. Why don't you take the comfortable chair?" Mr. Worthing put away a folder that he locked in the filing cabinet, which David presumed to be his information. While Mr. Worthing getting set, David nonchalantly pushed the other chair a couple of inches farther from the recliner. After another minute, Mr. Worthing gathered his things, walked around his desk, and sat down across from David.

"Sorry about that, David. I was very busy this morning and didn't have time to get everything situated. How are you doing today?"

David looked back at the man quizzically, thinking, Is there a certain way I should answer his questions? Mr. Worthing had his eyes trained on David. He did not blink or look away, which made his subject a little uneasy. David gathered his thoughts and replied, "Good, I think."

"Excellent, David. I just want to start off by getting to know each other. I'm not here to make you feel uncomfortable. If you do feel things are heading in that direction, please let me know. Sound good?" The teen nodded in agreement, not saying anything. "Great. I know there have been some problems for you socially here since you came into the high school. When I took my first job as a guidance counselor, I wanted to help kids like you, and that's still my main focus. I know what it's like to feel like kind of an outsider. I had my fair share of difficult times when I was your age, and hopefully you and I can share some stories, but we'll get to all that later. First, I thought we could have a discussion off the record. You know, just a little talk to get acquainted. I don't expect you to open up to me right away, someone you don't know at all, but I hope we can get there eventually. That okay with you?"

David had broken eye contact with Mr. Worthing halfway through his monologue and found himself looking past the man. "Yeah, that's fine with me."

"By the way, David, you can just call me Tyler or Ty. That 'Mr. Worthing' stuff makes me feel too old. I'm only 29, you know," he laughed. The counselor continued on to tell David all about himself, not recognizing just how uninterested David was in knowing that he was single and enjoyed jogging in his spare time. "What else is there I can tell you? This is the third learning institution I have worked in, so you could say I have diverse experience in different school districts."

The movement from school to school struck David as odd. Seeing the cynical look on the teen's face, Mr. Worthing explained that he had been looking for the right place to settle. The counselor continued trying to see if anything sparked the teen's interest so that he could build on any similarities. Nothing seemed to interest David, and it was obvious since he was looking anywhere but at the counselor. Finally, he knew he would have to resort to direct questioning.

"So, tell me about your family, David."

There was an uncomfortable pause as David thought about how he could describe his unorthodox family history. Mr. Worthing was about to interject, wondering if he had come on too strong, when David spoke.

"I'll say that my family is not like most kids'." David wanted to just get through the session and tell the man what he wanted to hear, but he had grown irritated.

"Most everyone in town knows about my family history. As a matter of fact, I'm sure you have it well documented in my file over there," David said nodding, his head in the direction of the filing cabinet. "I know you did your homework on me, Mr. Worthing, so let's not waste time. Is this the part where you want me to tell you how I felt about my family's incident and how life has been since? Is that what you want?"

David's sarcastic tone and blunt comments confounded the counselor. "Well, David, yes. Tell me a little about that. I'm here to listen. If it gets to be too much for you, just let me know. Go on, please."

David played with the fabric of his pants and thought about how he wanted to respond. He nonchalantly looked up at the clock and saw that there was only ten minutes left before his next class. Lucky for him, Mr. Worthing had taken up the majority of the time talking about himself in his attempt to ease into more personal discussion.

"Mr. Worthing, how is someone supposed to feel when one day your father and brother are walking out the door and the next thing you know they are gone for good? I know you want to know if I had guilt and all that. I can't swim, so what could I have done if even I had been there? I got through it in my own way and still do. It hit my mom hard as well, and our home life can be tough, but there is nothing I can do to change anything." He crossed his arms and stared at the wall. "I have to use the lav before my next class. Can I go now?"

The guidance counselor knew he was being stonewalled, but didn't want to push David since this was only their first session. Maybe this was a chance to gain some points with him.

"Okay, David, you can go. I'll see you the day after tomorrow, same time. Thanks for sharing."

"Whatever." The boy stalked out of the room.

Tyler Worthing moved his chair back to his desk and sat down. He put his head in his hands, knowing that if the rest of the sessions went like this one, his efforts would be fruitless.

CHAPTER 18

When David got home, his mom was eager to know how his first meeting with Mr. Worthing had gone. He brushed her off with a mumbled "okay" as he walked by and went upstairs. He knew he needed a little time to himself before yet another awkward dinner with his mother and Steve. David often wondered to himself why he did not just stay in his room rather than put himself through this daily ordeal. I already had to put up with one idiot today, he thought. But he knew that to keep his mom at ease, he would have to go along with her wishes, even if that meant tolerating Steve. Fortunately, Beth picked up on David's reluctance to discuss his day and did not ask her son any questions in front of his stepfather.

After their meal David retreated to the tranquility of his room, hoping his mom would not come asking about the counseling session. He began to replay the meeting with Mr. Worthing in his head. The more he thought about it, the more adverse he grew to the whole setup. He started to formulate a way he could approach these meetings in the future that would cost him the least amount of effort. While he had done his best to evade the guidance counselor's questions, he felt that the little information he had volunteered when he did answer was too much. The more I give him, the more he is going to want, he thought as he lay there. David grew increasingly irritated thinking about having to go through with these sessions. He knew that before he could fall asleep, he had to put his mind at ease. He got the shoebox.

David woke up Wednesday morning to the sound of rain peppering his windowpane. His first thought was of his meeting with Mr. Worthing. Angst welled up inside him. David understood he did not have much of a choice, but was not in the mood to have someone he barely knew judge him. All I have to do is get through a few more of these to pacify my mother, this jerk counselor and Mr. Mitchell.

His mother knocked and opened the door slightly. "David, I'll drive you to school today. You can throw your bike in the trunk if you want – the weather's supposed to clear up in the afternoon. Just hurry up and get ready, so I'm not late for work." Before leaving he checked his eye in the mirror. It was healing up much better than he thought it would. At least he had that going for him.

When the time came for his session, David was in a bad mood. He had just gotten a hard time from his teacher about missing a homework assignment. He slumped down in a chair in the counseling office and dropped his book bag on the floor with little care for its contents. Mr. Worthing's welcoming grin faded and his eyebrows rose. He knew by the young man's posture that he did not want to be here.

"Okay, David, something evidently is bothering you. What's up?"

The teenager mumbled something incoherent while propping his head up with his hand, his elbow on the arm of the chair.

"I'm sorry, what was that, David?"

Annoyed, the boy looked up at the counselor. "Not having a great day so far."

"Let me give you a few minutes to decompress, and I'll get some coffee." He picked up his mug and patted David on the shoulder as he walked by, shutting the door behind him.

The teen sat there, dreading the whole idea of the exercise and contemplated getting up and leaving. What could really happen? What's he going to do? David thought. Then he hesitated. This just may be a test to see if I'll leave if given the opportunity. I see what he's trying to do. This is all part of it. Another few minutes went by, and David almost dozed off. He jumped a little as the door swung open, and Mr. Worthing reappeared with a steaming cup of coffee.

107

"All right, David, hope that time to yourself has done you good. What's up?"

Over the next twenty minutes, the counselor attempted to jump-start some dialogue with open-ended questions, which David skillfully evaded. The back-and-forth conversation with the teen was generic and unproductive, and he could tell David was growing more and more aggravated. Although it was uncomfortable for David, he did take pleasure in frustrating Mr. Worthing and stonewalling his attempts to create a bond between them. He had no interest in calling him Tyler, as the man had suggested. This guy is worthless, he thought and almost laughed out loud. Mr. Worthless.

"Can I go use the bathroom?" The counselor seemed irked that the teen had interrupted his rambling monologue.

"Oh…well…sure, David."

David had planned this move to get out of the meeting as well as irritate Mr. Worthing. He bypassed the closest bathroom and continued down the hall. He knew of a back room in the gym used for excess storage where he could lie low. He had discovered it during gym class one day when he faked an injury to sit out and used that time to explore the old gymnasium. When he reached the spot, David glanced around to make sure no one was in sight before he slipped through the access door and plopped down on an old folded-up wrestling mat. He drifted in and out of sleep with a slight smile on his face, relishing the fact that he was ditching the session.

After some time, David looked up at the ticking clock and saw that he only had five minutes left until the period bell rang. He stretched and got up slowly, then made his way back to the office. On his walk back, David passed the lockers where Brock had pinned him up against the wall and finished him off with a punch to the gut. Anxiety rushed over him as he realized Brock would be back at school the next day. Had anyone been in the hall, they would have seen the shock on the teen's face. It crossed David's mind that, compared to Brock coming back, these sessions did not seem so bad after all.

David opened the office door as the period bell rang. He walked in holding his stomach, knowing that even Mr. Worthing would not question what took him so long.

"You okay, David? You look a little pale."

The teen reached down to grab his bag. "Yeah, I'm just not feeling well…must have been something I ate."

Mr. Worthing stood up. "Not a problem. If you're not feeling well, you're not feeling well. See you Friday?"

David nodded in affirmation and turned to exit.

"Oh, David, did you use the bathroom around the corner?" The teen stopped in his tracks, knowing that could only mean this guy had actually come looking for him.

"Uh, no. Under the circumstances I preferred to go to another bathroom that is not so frequently used, if you know what I mean. I went to the one by the gym." That should cover me if anyone saw me walk down that way.

"I went to check up on you and couldn't find you. Do you need to go home?"

The teen answered with a wave of the hand saying, "Nah, I'll be fine." He grinned, pleased that his feigned illness had gotten him out of this meeting.

When he got home, David dropped his bike in the driveway and hurried inside, as all he wanted was some solo time to think. However, Beth was eager to talk to her son, hoping the gamble she had taken on these counseling sessions would help him. Little did Beth know that she underestimated David's stubbornness and smarts in avoiding unwanted situations.

"Hi, David, how was school?"

"Okay, I guess," he answered as he tried to make a quick exit for his room.

"David, can't you give your mom a few minutes?" He slowly turned and moped his way back to the kitchen looking down at the worn pale yellow linoleum floor. "How is everything going with Ty…Mr. Worthing? He seems like such a nice man."

David felt like telling her what a waste of time the whole thing was. He thought to himself, Just tell her what she wants to hear. He faked half a smile as he spoke. "It's going fine, I guess. He seems okay. We've just been talking for a while, and I do feel a little better when I leave our meetings."

Beth smiled back at her son and pulled him in for a hug, wanting to believe him. "Oh, David, I think this is going to be good. I know it's been rough and some days are tougher than others, but stick with it and everything will be better in the future. You'll be glad that you did this when you look back on it, I swear. Brighter things are ahead."

David forced yet another smile. "Thanks, Mom." He went upstairs to relax and begin thinking of a plan to take care of his main problem – Brock.

He had been lying on his bed for an hour when he was startled by the sound of metal dragging on the ground, followed by the screech of tires. David knew what had just happened. Steve had plowed into his bike that he left in the driveway. His stepdad had complained to him before about leaving his bike in the driveway and had showed restraint in the past, but not today. A few seconds later, a car door slammed and he heard Steve yelling from the driveway.

"Damn it, David! What the hell is wrong with this kid?"

Beth opened the back door and met him. "What's the matter, Steve?"

"What's the matter? What's the matter, you're asking me? Can you not see what your son did here? How many times have we asked him not to leave his bike out? Damn thing scratched the front end of my Beamer when I hit it."

All Beth could do was try to calm him down since she figured David could hear this commotion. Beth looked at her husband with caring eyes. "Okay, he didn't do it on purpose. You know he's been having a rough time at school. It's just a habit he has to break."

"Having a tough time, huh? Well, guess what, we all have tough times. I have a tough time almost every day at the office. We have to teach him responsibility. I would do it, but David is not my son. He won't even give me the time of day. He basically ignores me and barely listens to you. Something has to change." Steve kicked the bike and began to pace. Beth looked away with tears in her eyes and briskly walked back inside. She slammed the back door behind her, leaving Steve by himself in the driveway.

Steve almost called out after her, but knew the damage had already been done and he did not care. He hopped back in his car, reversing it until the bike fell free. He got back out and tossed the bike off to the side. His stepfather had crushed the front tire with the bike frame bent beyond repair. David watched all this from his window. He softly said aloud, "I hate him."

David watched as the man he had come to despise pulled his car up in the driveway once again and walked slowly to the back door. Then he laid on the floor next to his vent trying to listen in on how things would transpire downstairs.

Coming in the door, Steve hung up his keys and laid his things on a kitchen chair. Beth was sitting at the dining room table with her head down. She was sobbing. He made his way over to her, putting his hand on her shoulder.

"I'm sorry. I had a bad day at the office and should not have said what I said. The bike just set me off and I…"

Looking up at him quickly with tired red eyes, she cut him off in an angry, hushed tone. "David most likely heard every word you said. How do you think he's feeling right now? I've been trying so hard to keep this family together but things keep falling apart."

Steve took a moment to mind his response so that he did not upset her any further. At the same time he resented being admonished by his wife every time he spoke his thoughts about the troubled teen. "I don't know what to say, Beth, except that I am sorry for upsetting you. You know I would never want to purposefully hurt your feelings. But I just feel I deserve more respect from your son. I don't understand how most of what happens between the two of us always comes back on me. We all have our bad days, and I'm allowed to have mine too."

Beth looked at her husband incredulously. "Did those words just come out of your mouth? He's a kid. He's in high school. He's trying, but you know there are some issues I am trying to work through with him right now. I would expect you to be more understanding regardless of how your day goes."

Steve threw up his hands. "I'm trying, Beth. You think I want it to be this way with David? Walk on eggshells in my own house? I feel like an outsider sometimes with the way you understand him and not me."

Beth got up from her chair knowing this conversation was going nowhere. She was getting more upset and could not believe what she was hearing. "You know what, Steve, have fun sleeping on the couch tonight, because I'm done with this. You are so selfish sometimes."

She walked towards the kitchen. Steve turned, thinking about stopping his wife, and Beth flinched.

"Don't," she said with a stern look on her face. She continued on into the kitchen. Steve quickly turned to head upstairs to get changed and pounded his fist on the banister, causing it to wobble.

In his room, David got up from the floor and smiled at the discord he had just heard. Knowing his mom, it would be a while before she forgave Steve. He could use this latest incident to his advantage. He grabbed a pad and pencil and started making notes for how to handle Brock at school, as well as cause some other collateral damage. His head was swimming with ideas. David knew the plan he had been mulling over would come together nicely if things went according to his scheme.

With Steve sulking in the basement, the rest of the night was quiet in the household. Around 8:00 p.m., David heard his mother make her way from the kitchen to the stairs. He assumed she was going to bed, so he shut off the light and pretended to be sleeping, hoping she would not bother to check on him. Beth stopped at her son's door, hesitating to knock, then turned and went to her bedroom.

A couple of hours later he could hear the light snore of his mother and the murmur of her bedroom television still on. David got out of bed and walked downstairs to grab something to eat. He went into the pantry and reached for a bag of butter pretzels when his stepfather's voice gave him a jolt.

"Hi David." The teenager dropped the pretzel bag in his surprise. He had not heard Steve come up the steps as he was rummaging through the pantry. David bent down to pick up the pretzels that had spilled on the floor without saying a word, but Steve continued on.

"I'm sorry. I didn't mean to frighten you. I thought you were your mother." David took his time cleaning up, choosing not to make eye contact with the man he loathed. Steve tried again. "You want me to make you something? You must have slept through dinner."

David thought to himself, What a fake. I've been trying to avoid you, you jerk. He straightened up and looked Steve in the eye. "Steve, do you really think I'm stupid? You don't think I heard what went on after you crushed my bike?" Steve shifted uncomfortably. He fumbled for words, but his surly stepson cut him off. "I heard everything you said. You know what, Steve? You and I haven't gotten along since day one. I never liked you and never will."

Steve was left standing there as David stormed out of the room feeling proud of himself for telling Steve exactly how he felt. Upstairs, the sound of the pretzels hitting the floor awoke Beth. She heard everything her son had to say. Beth buried her face in her pillow, weeping, now even more upset with Steve for deepening the rift with her son.

In the kitchen, Steve could hear the muffled crying of his wife upstairs. He made himself a scotch on the rocks, knowing full well he would not be welcome if he wanted to console her. He knew he would have to do something big to turn things around with Beth. Right now, he would just have to bide his time and wait for the perfect moment.

CHAPTER 19

The next day David's mom knocked on his door, awakening her son. "Good morning," she said as she sat on the bed. "I know you probably heard Steve and me exchange words last night. I'm sorry about your bike, but your birthday is right around the corner, so maybe I can work something out for you, okay?"

David sat up and rubbed his eyes. "Sure."

Beth stood as she patted her son's head. "I can drive you to school today unless you would rather take the bus."

David thought for a few seconds. He realized with Brock back from suspension, it would be best if he skipped the bus for a while. "Um, yeah, I'll take a ride."

"All right, be downstairs in a half-hour please."

Beth kept conversation with her son to a minimum on the way to school, not wanting to dwell on the subject of what had occurred the night before. The last thing she wanted was for David to lash out at her the way he had with Steve.

After being dropped off, David went about his daily routine, glad that today did not include another session with the guidance counselor. "Maybe things aren't so bad after all. He can't make me say anything. If I keep frustrating this guy, he has to give up at some point, even though he doesn't want to look bad in Mr. Mitchell's eyes," he thought.

With only two hours left in the school day, the sudden sight of Brock approaching shattered David's good feeling. It was too late to turn back, so he kept walking in the direction of his next class at the end of the corridor. As he moved closer to his adversary, he felt like everything was in slow motion. He could hear people whispering as they noticed the two closing in on each other.

Brock was talking to Joe Follson and did not see David until they were only a few yards apart. Students at their lockers turned to look in anticipation of another altercation. David did not even glance in Brock's direction and moved as close to the opposite side of the hallway as he could. Brock stared him down as he passed.

"Only a matter of time," he snarled.

Mr. Gavin stood watch nearby, shaking his head in disgust. Kids lingered, hoping something would occur, but David meekly skirted the bully. He felt that nervousness in the pit of his stomach once again and knew that he would have to do something before he took another pounding. Either I take care of the situation or they're going to take care of me, he thought.

The next day David had his mother drop him off at school again. Without his bike David's best option was getting a ride rather than taking the bus or walking. He did not know where Brock was planning to ambush him, but they were not going to catch David alone and vulnerable again if he could help it.

Soon it came time for another uncomfortable meeting with Mr. Worthing. David savored watching the guidance counselor grow frustrated as he tried many tactics to get him to open up. Nothing seemed to work as David refused to cooperate.

David was not like any pupil Mr. Worthing had worked with before. Nothing seemed to faze him, which bewildered the man. The counselor had become preoccupied thinking about David and how he could somehow get through to him. He could not voice his frustrations to anyone, as he did not want to seem ineffective to his boss. The principal had entrusted him with this special assignment, and the counselor could not let him down with so much at stake.

After a long fruitless conversation, the man's annoyance grew to the point that he had to excuse himself to take a break. Never in his career had a student shut him out like this. He had tried every technique he knew to get something, anything from the boy. At first he had not minded the small talk, but now it was just ridiculous how openly David was resisting him. I can't force him to talk, the man thought as he walked down the hallway with his hands in his pockets. At that moment, the principal turned the corner and almost ran into him.

"Whoa! Excuse me, Tyler." The counselor could not immediately find words for a response since he was deep in thought regarding the enigma sitting in his office. The principal furrowed his brow and asked, "Are you okay?"

"Oh, ah, yeah, yeah. No, everything is fine. Sorry, I didn't see you there. I'm just thinking about something."

The principal looked at the counselor quizzically and then at his watch. "Well, isn't David in your office right now?"

Tyler Worthing could feel his face growing red. "Yes, of course. You know, he really is a good kid. Solid conversations we've had so far. I just needed to use the bathroom. Too much coffee, you know?" he nervously chuckled, wishing his boss would appreciate the joke.

"Well, I'm looking forward to hearing about the progress you've made. You haven't given me much so far. Remember, we've got to keep an eye on him. If anything happens…" The principal didn't have to finish his sentence for the counselor to catch the insinuation.

"Absolutely, sir. I fully understand." As they parted company, the principal turned and looked back at the man with a shake of his head. He walked by the guidance office and peered in as the door was ajar. He noticed a cola can on the desk and saw that the office was vacant with no sign of David. The principal paused for a moment and then continued on, hoping there was a good explanation.

Tyler walked into the men's bathroom with his mind racing after the run-in with the principal. He was completely frazzled as he sensed his superior did not believe a word he had said about his progress with

117

David. He was growing paranoid. Did Mitchell regret hiring him? He had to do something to fix this. He couldn't face losing a third job in the span of five years.

He stared into the mirror for a minute and splashed some water on his face. After drying his face with a paper towel, he looked at his watch and saw he had been gone for five minutes. He speed-walked back to his office to discover it was empty. He could only hope that Roy Mitchell would not find out.

David had sought sanctuary in the old gym again, resting for a little while until the bell rang. He took pleasure in knowing that Mr. Worthing did not know how to handle him. While David was sure the whole meeting concept was the principal's idea, he enjoyed watching the guidance counselor struggle. He would eventually discover that any person who tried to change David would face an unwavering opponent.

"Hi, David. How was your day?" Beth asked. He got into the car, tossing his backpack into the back seat.

"Not bad, really." Beth started asking about the session with Mr. Worthing, but as David looked out the window he saw Brock and his two minions, Sean and Joe, walking across the front lawn of the high school. The three teens were laughing and talking, and Sean nudged one small kid out of the way as they strolled away from school. Brock looked up and met David's eye as Joe and Sean kept talking. David's eyes grew wide as Brock drew his finger across his throat.

"David, did you hear me?" David turned to his mother, not realizing how worried he looked. "What's wrong?"

"Nothing, Mom. Sorry, I was just thinking about something." He knew Brock was going to come at him soon and that he had to be ready.

When they pulled in the driveway, Beth said, "I have a present for you, honey. Stay right here." He watched as she walked around the corner of the house towards the garage. David heard the garage door open and then saw his mom reappear, waving him over. "Okay, come on over here," she said excitedly.

David got out of the car and walked over to his mom. Sitting in the open garage propped up with its kickstand was a brand new black and silver BMX bike.

"Happy early birthday!" his mother exclaimed, clasping her hands. David stood with his jaw slack then managed a slight grin. After he broke from his admiration, he looked at his mother.

"Wow! Thanks, Mom." She walked over with tears in her eyes and hugged her son. She had not seen him this happy in a long time. David walked around his new bike, running his hands over the seat, down the back tire, back up the frame and across the handlebars.

"Well, sweetie, are you going to stand there admiring it or ride it? I took a half-day from work and asked the man at the bike shop what the biggest seller was these days."

"Mom, this is like the best bike out there. I've seen other kids with them, but never thought..." His words trailed off as he looked at his bike head-on in awe. "This just blows away my other bike. Not even on the same level."

Beth smiled at her son and patted him on the shoulder. "I'm really happy you like it, and I'm really sorry about your other bike. I know you had a lot of memories on that one."

David just continued to stare at his bike, barely listening to what his mother was saying. "No problem, Mom."

"Now don't be gone too long. I'll expect you back in about an hour." She walked inside and left David alone with his new prized possession.

He wasted no time hopping on his bike and speeding down the driveway. He could not believe how different it felt from his old one. This handles better, is faster, and looks way cooler than my other bike. Thanks, Steve, you idiot. He rode off as fast as he could go down the street in the direction of The Shadows.

On the way to his destination, David thought about the plan he had been concocting for Brock. He was well aware that he would need to enlist the help of others. Eugene was one person he knew would be good, but he also knew the homeless man would not knowingly be a part of a high school feud. I'll just have to come up with something to entice him, David thought. He lifted off his seat and pedaled faster with his bike gleaming in the sunlight. He rode up the short access road that led to the old water treatment plant and did a double take when he saw a large sign standing tall in a patch of grass next to the gate.

COMMERCIAL LAND SALE – 10.4 ACRES

He jumped off his bike. He took in the sight before him and pondered what might happen to this land in the not too distant future. David laid his bike down and walked over to the sign. He tried to push it over, but it was too heavy, being staked into the ground and weighted with sandbags. He would have to come back later and take care of it. If no one can read the sign, they won't know it's for sale. This could be just what I need to convince Eugene to help me.

David picked up his bike and made his way through the open field. The homeless man's campsite was vacant, which told David that he had to be fishing. The teen leaned his brand new bike against a tree and strolled toward the river. He caught sight of his friend and cautiously walked over the unsteady rocks of the bank towards the man. "Eugene! Hey, what's going on?"

The weathered man gave him a wave and then quickly grabbed the rod with his free hand as the tip dipped down to the water. He frantically reeled in his potential catch.

"Damn!" he exclaimed as his line went limp. "Sucker got away. I'll get him though, I'll get him." He reeled in the rest of his line and picked up his lone catch of the day. He turned to the boy and walked across the rocks. "Hey, David. How's it going today?"

David told him about the "For Sale" sign he had seen next to the access road. "Once that sells, they are probably going to take down the woods next," David said with concern in his voice.

The vagabond looked back at David, trying to think while he spoke. "Settle down, boy, settle down. They can't come down here and clear all the trees just like that," Eugene said, snapping his fingers. "Besides, the way development is going nowadays, these woods are not going to be standing forever. They won't take them all down, but there will come a day when your town will grow and encroach on this area. I can't stay here forever."

David looked back at him in anger and confusion. "It sounds like you want to give up without even trying. What's wrong with you, Eugene? Don't you care about this place? This is your home as much as it is my home away from home. We have to do something!"

Eugene laughed. "You need to relax, David. What I mean is, it's not going to happen overnight, but there's not much two people can do to stop them. I do care about this place and never want to see environments ruined, but there will come a point that I have to move on. That's what I have been doing for a long time now."

The teenager was silent as he walked ahead towards his new bike. Eugene felt bad that he had apparently let him down. "David, if you really care about this place and want to do something, we can raise some hell. If you find out they are coming down here to do some surveying, we can make it tough on them and perhaps delay the inevitable. But keep in mind that it would also force me to move on quicker, since it would bring on some heat." He paused. "Look, if you want to fight back, I'm in. After all, you've been nice to me and understand me for who I am. I appreciate that."

David turned with a big smile on his face. "That's great. Thanks, Eugene. I gotta run home for dinner, but I'll find out more details and will be back to plan this out with you." He picked up his bike and walked it along the trail, giving Eugene a wave.

"Nice bike!" Eugene yelled after him.

David rode past the "For Sale" sign on his way home. Won't be up for sale if I can help it.

Later on in his room, David picked up the phone and called his buddy Aaron. He spoke quietly since his mother had never approved of this acquaintance. "Hi, Aaron, it's David. Listen, I need your help with something next Saturday. It has to do with those guys at school I've had trouble with." He told Aaron about what he had come up with so far.

"Does your goody-goody friend Michelle know about this?" Aaron asked.

"No, I have not talked to her in a while."

"Good, because you don't need her ruining it."

"Relax Aaron, I realize you do not like her."

After a few more minutes of conversation David hung up and went back to his grand plan. He jotted down a few more notes and tried to think of who else could assist him. He would need all the help he could get to pull it off. He would also have to take a major personal risk. He recognized that he would need to give Brock what he wanted – a chance to fight him. But if his plan came to fruition, it would take care of the major source of anxiety in his life. Before he went to bed, David set his alarm for 1:30 a.m.

After a few hours of solid sleep, he awoke to his alarm faintly sounding, as he had turned down the volume so his mom or Steve did not wake. He dressed and slipped out the window. David grabbed his new bike, which he had purposely left in the backyard for an easy getaway, and made off down the cold, quiet street.

He had some time to think on his way and kept off the roads, which made for a nice leisurely ride down the sidewalks. What would next weekend bring? What were the chances his plan would completely backfire? By the end of the ride, he had convinced himself he had no choice but to carry out his plan and that tomorrow would be the first phase of his preparation. He rode up the access road and pulled over into the grass where he stood face to face with the "For Sale" sign. He laid his bike down behind a tree and looked around to make sure he was alone.

First, David removed the ten heavy sandbags that weighed down the sign. He then proceeded to rock the sign back and forth until the stakes loosened. After it was leaning, David took a run at it and jumped into the wooden facade shoulder first. The sign sagged and needed one more blow to knock it down. He took a second run at it, and the sign fell to the ground with a muffled thud. David grabbed a heavy rock with two hands and began smashing the sign until the wording was indiscernible.

After he got in a dozen solid blows, he noticed the sound was echoing down the street. Good thing there weren't any houses nearby. David stepped back, breathing heavily, and assessed the damage. The phone number was illegible and the sign itself was almost completely defaced with splintered holes. He smiled. No sign, no information, no sale.

CHAPTER 20

Saturday morning David woke up refreshed, looking forward to talking with Eugene. He saw that Steve's car was not in the driveway and figured he was out playing golf, since it was a nice day. He took advantage of the opportunity to watch TV in the basement while eating a bowl of cereal. After lying around for a while, he went back upstairs where his mom was folding laundry in her bedroom. "I'm going to head out for a little while, Mom. I'll be back," he muttered in her direction.

"Okay. Just be home in time for dinner."

David washed up and gathered his things, including the plans he had drawn up for Brock's ambush. By noon he was speeding down the street looking up at the ominous clouds that signaled an impending storm.

When he reached the access road, he looked off to the side smiling at the sign he had demolished the night before. David surveyed the area around the vacant water treatment plant to familiarize himself with the immediate surroundings of the building. Mapping out his scheme over the past few days had given him a good idea of where everything would take place, but being down here on site really gave him a clear perspective.

He walked his bike over to the plant stairs, his starting point. Leaning his bike on the railing he looked at the random objects that people discarded next to the building. Townspeople used this location to illegally dump junk they did not want to pay to have hauled off. Things like refrigerators, tables, mattresses, and even a couch littered the far side of the plant. Along with the junk, debris left over from plant operations was scattered about. Wooden pallets, a few large truck tires, crates, and some scrap metal lay around exposed to the elements. The tires were starting to crack from dry rot, the crates and pallets were coming apart, and the metal was rusted.

David's mind wandered as he looked over these objects, knowing he could put this worthless trash to his own good use. I could build up a barrier so they can't get to me. That's how I'll be able to make my escape to the woods. David did not want to waste any time and quickly got to work dragging the items into place. After a period of nonstop heavy labor, his blockade began to take shape as it extended out from the steps of the plant. He rolled the tires over and clumsily stacked them by pushing them over one on top of the other.

David continued to haul the debris over to his line of defense until the arrangement satisfied him. The stability of the structure was paramount so that it could withstand a possible assault from Brock, Sean and Joe. If any of them caught him before he made it to the woods, David would be in big trouble. He stood back and tried to envision the confrontation starting in this area, taking into account any possible moves that could be made. David picked out the exact spot he would stand when Brock came down that day, behind the stacked pallets next to the tires. He found a small length of metal pipe on the ground and placed it into the casing of one of the tires, figuring it might come in handy if something went wrong.

David traced his trek down into the woods to make sure there were no rocks or anything else that might trip him up. He cleared away a few shrubs right near the crest of the hill he planned on descending leading to the rigged trail in the belly of The Shadows. He turned back and admired his work. He just hoped it would prove practical for his purposes. The teen felt confident that the route he had walked would lead him to the safety of the woods. No one knows this place like I do, he thought. If his initial strategy was successful and they followed him into The Shadows, it would trigger the ultimate payback.

Now it was time to get Eugene on board. As he approached the campsite, he saw Eugene sitting on a rock near the fire. At the sound of his steps, the vagrant looked

125

his way and fumbled to hide something under his jacket. He jumped up and staggered into his tent out of view. David heard the slam of the wooden trunk where Eugene kept his personal effects. Weird, David thought. "Hey, Eugene. How's it going?" he called.

Eugene stumbled from the tent. "Hey, David," he slurred. "Almost didn't see you there." The man's comment confused David. He was sure they had made eye contact when David walked into the camp. Maybe he was having an off day. "What're you doin' down here today?"

The teen gave the obviously disoriented man a curious look. "Uh, Eugene, I was down here yesterday. Remember our talk?" The homeless man stared at him blankly. The teen continued on. "Eugene, I took care of that "For Sale" sign last night, but someone must already be interested because word has it they will be down here next Saturday. My stepdad told me that surveyors will be checking out the woods to see what they want to tear down." David felt a little guilty lying to this man who had become a friend of sorts, but he figured Eugene would understand in the end.

The hobo scratched his nappy beard thoughtfully. "Oh, right. Now I remember..."

How this man could forget a conversation that had occurred not even twenty-four hours earlier perplexed David. "Eugene, I would just need your help setting up a few traps. Are you with me on this?"

Eugene's eyes were glassy and his pupils were pinpoints, but he mustered an answer. "Sure, I'm with you. Just tell me what you want me to do."

David looked around the campsite to see what, if anything, the vagrant had that could be useful. "Well, my plan is to be down here and wait for them to arrive by the old water treatment plant. I'll hopefully have a couple friends down here in the woods to keep an eye out while others will be up there watching me from the brush. You've already seen my one buddy down here, so you'll recognize

Patrick when you see him." Eugene just nodded as David rambled on with his proposal.

"You can stay here at your campsite. I'll head up to the plant and try to raise enough of a ruckus to disturb their operations. I figure the traps are a safety precaution in case they come after us. I want to make it as rough as possible for them if they are crazy enough to chase me. Do you have anything down here we might be able to use, like a shovel or something?"

The vagrant took a moment to process the question and then looked around his camp. He glanced at the big log behind him, and his eyes opened as much as his present condition allowed. "You wouldn't believe what I pick up on my travels. If I can carry it, it's comin' with me," he answered, continuing to slur. Eugene slowly shuffled his way over to the large, heavy log. David helped him rock it back and forth until it rolled a couple feet, revealing a rectangular furrow dug into the earth. A shovel, an extra tarp, and some scrap metal occupied the depression. "There," Eugene said, pointing down. "Knew I had something."

David reached down and grabbed the shovel. "Okay, Eugene, you want to help me or you too tired today?"

The impaired man slowly waved his hand. "Nah, I'm not feeling all that well right now. Why don't you get started without me?" David began to walk in the direction of the planned-out area. "Traps!" Eugene suddenly yelled.

The man who had seemed half-asleep during their conversation startled the teen.

"What?"

Eugene cupped his hands around his mouth saying, "Traps, you want to make traps, right?" David nodded his head in affirmation.

"Holes, dig holes. A series of them. Maybe even a pit, tripwire, ya know? You have a good imagination. When you're finished lemme know and I'll take a look. I have some experience." Eugene slumped down on the log as if what he had just voiced had drained any remaining energy out of him. He leaned over the log trying to balance himself with his hands before standing and then threw up. Eugene turned back to David, giving a thumbs up with mucus dripping from his lips.

David turned away quickly in disgust, gagging at the sight of the man. "Thanks!" he yelled back. He trudged on through The Shadows shaking his head at the mess of a man he left behind. It was time to focus on the task at hand. Nervousness swept over him as he thought about next weekend. David knew there was a serious chance the entire snare could fail. What if things went wrong? What if one of those guys caught him before he made it to The Shadows?

David walked along the seldom-used path thinking about school, home, his father, his mother, and his brother. He was interrupted from his introspection when he caught a blur out of the corner of his eye, just to his left up on a rise. Already feeling paranoid, David called out, "Who's there?" The abrupt sight of his buddy Patrick spooked David as he turned. "Holy crap, man, you scared me!"

"Relax, dude. When did you get so uptight?"

David walked past his friend, still consumed by his own thoughts. "I just have a lot on my mind, Patrick. By the way, where've you been?"

"Well, David, it's kind of tough to show your face when the police want to question you for something one of your friends told them about."

David looked sheepish and hesitated before he spoke. "Sorry, man, but what was I supposed to do? The cops were convinced I nailed Brock." It was quiet for a moment as David stared at the ground, kicking a few rocks. "Look, Patrick, I'm planning something you may want to be a part of. It'll teach those guys a lesson. They're the ones who started everything. You saw it yourself."

"What are you thinking?"

David told Patrick about his plan, the traps he had in mind, and the timing of it all.

"I'm in," Patrick said. "Those punks deserve everything they get."

"All right then, I'll see you here next Saturday, early."

"Sounds good, see you then," Patrick answered. He disappeared into the thickets as fast as he had shown up.

David had walked too far down the trail with Patrick and backtracked until he reached the entrance from the field that was his starting point. Looking down the path, he saw a grouping of trees that would be a good spot for his first trap. He took his hand-drawn map out of his backpack and assessed the landscape ahead of him. This will be perfect, he thought. David struck one of the trees with the shovel a few times to mark it. For the next twenty minutes he piled rocks next to the trees in preparation for his trap.

David put down the last rock and lifted his arm to wipe his brow. "Ouch!" he blurted out. He had caught his forearm on a sticker bush. He saw that a couple of thorns had torn through his shirt and sliced a small gash in his skin. He put his arm to his mouth and sucked the blood, contemplating the thorn bush.

Next, he walked down the trail until he found a good area to set his second snare. He dug a hole just the right size to catch someone's foot in, then did the same thing on the other side of the trail to mark the starting point of the trap. He moved on along the trail until he was fairly close to Eugene's camp and scraped the shovel on the ground until he had made a roughly fifteen-foot-long trench that stretched across the path. David had an idea for this last location but would definitely need help to get this all finished in time for next weekend.

When David finished, he walked over to Eugene who was lying on a fallen tree trunk sleeping. "Hey, Eugene." David lightly tapped the man on the thigh with the shovel. Eugene awoke slowly, appearing disoriented as he slurped up his drool. David sat down on the log next to him as Eugene righted himself.

"Okay, boy, okay. What's going on?"

David made sure he had the homeless man's attention as he pointed to the trench he had just outlined. "See that, Eugene? That's the last one. I need you to dig it out as deep as you can."

Eugene nodded and David got up to leave when he noticed a long, thick rope lying in the leaves off to the side. "I'm gonna to borrow your rope, if you don't mind. After I take care of this one last thing, I have to head home. I'll be back down later on this week to finish everything up." A nod was all the wasted man could muster as the teen walked away.

David looked up the steep incline to the side of the clearing, concentrating on a tree that leaned over Eugene's encampment. He looked around until he found a large chunk of broken-off stump that was splintered on one side. He tied the rope around it then plodded up the steep rise and laid the rope and heavy stump next to the tree he had identified as his anchor. He fastened the other end of the rope to a branch that leaned over the edge of the bluff. When the teen was content with the setup, he trotted back down the hill, waved to Eugene and headed for his bike. Eugene lay back down and drifted off to sleep.

CHAPTER 21

David retreated to his room after dinner with his mother, while Steve stayed put in the basement. He was eager to add more details to the mapped-out plans that he had drawn the prior evening. Now that he had built up the barrier by the plant and started the traps, David could expand on his ideas. He wanted to refine his scheme to be as foolproof and simple, yet effective, as possible.

David redrew maps of the areas where he thought most of the action would take place. The first area was the plot of land adjacent to the defunct water treatment facility, which he marked as "The Plant" at the top of the paper. David would be waiting there for Brock along with what he imagined to be numerous kids from school looking to see a fight. In order to get Brock, Sean and Joe to chase him into the woods, David would need to do something to initiate a response. David had already walked off the best route to take into the woods by way of the embankment. All he could do was hope he had enough of a head start to get away and that the descent into the woods would slow down his pursuers. I guess I'll just have to see how it plays out before I know what to do.

That brought him to the next map, which he had labeled as "The Trail." This booby-trapped labyrinth would be David's chance to get back at the bullies one by one if all his snares worked properly. Brock was the biggest of the boys, and David figured he was also probably the slowest, which would work out in this instance. With Sean and Joe being the lackeys, David surmised Brock would expect those two to get him. He knew Brock wanted this fight badly and needed it to happen in front of a lot of people to restore his damaged reputation.

After he finished up the other sketches, he knew the final obstacle had to be his best in case the others did not go as planned. David drew the area leading up to Eugene's campsite, with which he had grown very familiar. He made a box on the path that represented a pit that he planned on filling with muck from the riverbank.

David thought for a minute about how he could make this last snare multifaceted, as this had to be his fail-safe. David figured that there was a possibility the first two traps could scare them off, but he could not take any chances. With the three of them hunting him down, David presumed they would be so consumed with catching him they might not even notice the traps they were running into. He was not as focused on Sean and Joe – his main concern was Brock.

Next, he worked on strategizing the best place for his accomplices to hide out in The Shadows. He looked over the names he had written down on his first blueprint knowing that Eugene should stay by his tent. David thought Patrick and Aaron were street smart enough to know what to do while hiding in the brush. The last name David had written down was Luke with a question mark. He did not know what to expect from him. Luke had already proven to be unpredictable and might be a risk, but David needed all the reinforcements he could gather just in case. Out of all of them, Luke would definitely want to get back at these guys since they have terrorized him too. But I'll have to really contemplate that one. He would have to show me he can be trusted, especially with something as important as this. He put his project off to the side and laid back with his hands behind his head, smiling at the prospect of carrying out his plan.

On Monday, when the time came for his appointment with Mr. Worthing, David was so tired of going through the motions that he barely made any effort during the session. From the beginning he never really understood what Mr. Worthing was trying to get out of him. He could tell the desperate guidance counselor was making every effort he could to get him to crack and spill out his emotions. David took grim pleasure in the fact that the man before him was getting so upset that he had raised his voice a few times while probing the teen for any fragment of personal revelation.

David got up from the chair as the bell rang, giving the counselor a nod as he left the office. Mr. Worthing dropped the pencil he was holding and squeezed the bridge of his nose, fighting off a developing headache.

The day ended as it had begun for David, without incident. He walked through the halls looking at some streamers cascading from a hand-painted poster hanging that read 'Class of 1986.' I can't wait to graduate and get out of this dump. He tore a blue streamer off the sign and dropped it to the floor.

Outside, he walked over to the bike rack and noticed his back tire was flat. It appeared that someone had slashed it, as the slit was too clean to have happened on his ride in – he would have noticed it. He heard the honk of a car horn and saw a black Chevy IROC driving away. Brock's hand extended out the passenger-side window giving the middle finger and cackles emanated from the vehicle. David knew he had no recourse, for to get the school or his mother involved could doom his plans for the weekend.

He walked his bike all the way home, which took almost an hour. Entering the kitchen, David could tell he worried his mother, who was on the brink of tears.

"Where have you been?"

"I got a flat on the way home, Mom. I tried to get home as soon as possible since I knew you would be worried."

"David, I'm sorry, but you have to understand. Those boys scare me considering what has already happened."

"It was just a flat. Nothing to worry about."

She hugged her son, trying to keep her emotions in check. "I love you, honey."

Upstairs, Steve had heard the panic in his wife's voice. He rushed downstairs with his dress shirt untucked and unbuttoned and stepped into the kitchen.

"Beth, why don't I take the bike to get looked at tomorrow during my lunch break? I can pick it up later on after work," Steve said. Beth and David both looked surprised not knowing how to react at first.

David smirked. And there it is, a desperate attempt to make things right by a desperate man.

"Well, that's really nice of you to offer," Beth replied. She then turned to her son. "How does that sound, David? I could drive you to school tomorrow."

Looking to get out of the awkward situation quickly, David nodded in agreement. "Sure."

The next morning as Steve loaded David's bike into the trunk of his car, he caught a glimpse of the laceration on the tire. He had overheard David tell his mother that it had occurred on the way home, but clearly someone had slashed the tire intentionally with a blade. "This is too cleanly cut to be mistaken for something else. What is this kid trying to hide?" he said with a shake of his head.

David watched as his stepfather backed out of the driveway. He had been looking out his bedroom window while Steve inspected the tire. He could tell from Steve's body language that he was skeptical of how he claimed the tire sustained the damage. If he tries to say anything to my mom it would be his word versus mine. I know he won't risk that.

Tuesday was very mundane for David. No one bothered him and for once he seemed to be able to lie low. Any day I am not pestered by anyone or called on by teachers is a good day to me. When he spotted Mr. Worthing down the hallway the anxiety hit David for the first time all day. Today, however, they did not have a session scheduled and the teen did not want to have any more interaction with the guidance counselor than required. He simply went back around the corner and wasted a few minutes making himself look busy until the counselor had left the area.

Across the hallway, Mr. Gavin was observing David, noticing his reaction to seeing Tyler. The hall monitor felt bad for the teen. This kid is tortured enough here at school and now is being subjected to meetings with Tyler Worthing? Mr. Gavin regarded the counselor as pretentious.

After his last class David went to his locker, gathered all his things and went outside where his mother was waiting for him in the parking lot. David looked around for any sign of Brock but did not sense any trouble. It was unnerving to have to live his life in constant fear, but he hoped the weekend would change all of that.

When David and his mother pulled up the driveway, there sat his bike, propped up on its kickstand just like when he first had laid eyes on it. Steve emerged from the garage holding a rag in one hand and waving with the other with a forced smile. "Hey there. I figured I would clean it up since it had some mud on it. The guy at the store said it's good to go."

David walked over and smiled, which Steve noticed. Beth appeared very happy as well, walking up behind her son and touching him on the shoulder.

As much as it hurt him to do it, David forced himself to say, "Thanks."

Steve wiped his hands on the rag. "Don't mention it, pal." David turned away and rolled his eyes. Beth and Steve walked into the house as David took his bike for a quick spin around the block. Even if Steve had used the repair job as a ploy to make his own repairs on his relationship with his wife having his new bike back thrilled David.

The following day David locked his bike up at a rack on a different side of the school. After his fourth class of the morning, it was time for another scheduled meeting with Mr. Worthing. David walked into the counselor's office to find him smiling and in a good mood. The man's pleasant demeanor struck David as odd since Mr. Worthing had been showing blatant signs of dissatisfaction during their last couple of get-togethers.

Mr. Worthing stood up upon seeing the student. "Hey, David, how's it going today?"

"Fine," David answered. Being that the recliner was occupied with paperwork and files he sat in the straight-backed chair. As he sat David noticed two cans of cola sitting on the desk.

"These sodas are warm. Why don't you go down and grab some ice and two plastic cups from the cafeteria? Just tell them I sent you."

"Okay," David unenthusiastically replied. He walked out of the office and down the hall, taking his time. *I guess a free soda ain't so bad.* David reached the cafeteria and asked the attendant for cups and ice.

"This is for Mr. Worthing, you say?" the hairnetted woman asked.

"Yeah." The woman rolled her eyes. *Seems I'm not the only one annoyed with this guy.*

When David returned to the office Mr. Worthing was sitting at his desk reading the newspaper with his feet up. "Just catching up on some sports here. Do you follow any of the teams?"

David gave the counselor a bland look, knowing he was making another weak effort to establish a connection. "Not really."

"Well, not everyone is a sports fan. All right, put those cups down. I already opened up the cans, so enjoy."

What a weirdo. Who does that? David sat back and drank his soda as Mr. Worthing began droning on, asking questions about how school was going. As before, David did his best to deflect and give short answers. For some reason the counselor did not seem to get as frazzled with the parrying as he had in the past.

After about ten minutes, David began to feel tired and dizzy. His head drooped and his eyes half closed. He could not shake the overwhelming lethargy he was experiencing. Mr. Worthing looked concerned and stood up, staring at David intensely.

"Are you all right, David? What's wrong?"

The teen held onto the chair to stabilize himself and slurred, "I don't know. Not … feeling … right." He dropped the cup as the last little bit of soda and half melted ice cubes spilled onto the floor.

Mr. Worthing rushed over and cleared off the papers and a few accordion files that he had calculatingly placed on his lounge chair this morning. "Okay, okay, let's get you over here so you can lie back," he said as he helped David to the chair. He reclined the chair as David's eyes blinked and struggled to stay open.

Mr. Worthing sat back down watching the teen and then looked at his watch. He deliberated for a few minutes. Am I potentially making a big mistake here with David like I have with other students in the past? He cupped his hands up to his mouth and took a deep breath. It's now or never. Get on with it, Tyler. This is intended to help.

CHAPTER 22

Tyler Worthing reached into his pocket and took out his keys, unlocking his desk drawer. He pulled out a black leather-backed notepad, a gold-tinted pen, a tape recorder, and a book titled Advanced Techniques of Sleep Hypnosis. He had earmarked several pages in the book in anticipation of this moment. Desperate times call for desperate measures. Besides, no student is better suited for this type of experiment than David Collie. This could revolutionize what Principal Mitchell is working toward. He opened the book and began poring over the copious notes he had made in the margins.

After a few minutes of review he pulled up a chair next to David, turned on the tape recorder, and readied the notepad on his lap. The counselor started off with a few test hypnotic phrases to try and elicit a subconscious response from the teen. David merely groaned. He seemed to be in a deep sleep and was not receptive. Tyler nudged the teen to stir him and then tried again with more hypnosis-speak. He attempted to get the right tone and volume in his voice to evoke a reaction from David.

"Tell me about your childhood, David. What was it like?" Mr. Worthing continued probing, changing the inflection of his voice with each phrase. "Tell me about your father and your brother."

After a few more minutes without a response, Mr. Worthing tilted his head back in frustration. Why did I do this? With his sudden movement the notepad slipped off his lap, slapping to the floor.

David flinched. The counselor froze, trying to think of a way to explain this situation should the teen wake. David squirmed and mumbled a few incoherent words, but did not open his eyes. Then he spoke in a hushed voice, "I loved my dad and my brother. I miss them."

The counselor's mouth fell open in amazement. He moved both his chair and the recorder closer. When

David's words trailed off, he started asking the teen more questions. Some provoked more of a response than others, such as those related to his childhood. He made note of what inquiries and hypnosis techniques were successful as David verbalized personal feelings in his hypnotic state. The teen I think I just unlocked this boy. He grinned proudly.

After about a half-hour he counselor halted the session and his subject fell silent. He put away the recorder, notepad, and hypnosis book as he sat back down at his desk, then spoke quietly to the boy. "David, you will awake in five minutes and have no recollection of our conversation." Five minutes later David opened his eyes and strained to sit up from the recliner, still foggy.

Mr. Worthing was busying himself with some other files on his desk. "Good, you're up," he said, looking over at the student. "The nurse just left and said you probably are fatigued."

David appeared puzzled. "Huh? Oh, I don't know. I guess. I can't believe I just fell asleep like that. It's really never happened before."

The counselor looked at him seriously. "Have you had trouble sleeping lately, David? It's understandable."

David, always the one to deflect and think of the easiest way out, replied in a tired voice. "No, no. I mean yes, I haven't been sleeping that great."

Mr. Worthing nodded, knowing he was giving the teen a way of explaining himself. "Okay, that's what the nurse thought. Do you want me to call your mom?"

David did not want her in his business more than she already was. "No thanks. I don't think that's necessary."

The counselor stood up. "Okay. The nurse didn't think it was a major concern. Try and rest up. I'll see you on Friday."

David collected himself and rubbed his eyes. "Okay."

Before the guidance counselor shut the office door, he said, "Don't worry, David, I won't tell anyone about your falling asleep. I try to keep my meetings as confidential as possible, so I will tell the nurse to keep quiet too."

David nodded in appreciation as he walked away, but now he was nervous about having to go by the nurse's station on the way to his locker. As he walked quickly by the nurse's door, he saw a sign: Out to Lunch – Back at 1 p.m. The period bell rang and he glanced at the caged clock on the wall. 12:55. Weird. As he stood there confused, the nurse walked up.

"Excuse me dear." She fumbled for her keys and unlocked the door. "Do you need something or are you just here for a visit?" She smiled.

David eyed her suspiciously. "No, I'm okay. Thanks." The nurse looked quizzically at him as he walked away.

David felt lightheaded the rest of the day and was far more mentally removed from his classes than normal. One of his teachers asked if he was feeling all right, but for the most part everyone else just shrugged off his strange behavior as David being himself.

Walking the halls to his last class, David bumped into a couple of students in his dizzied state as he made his way through the crowd. Then he came in contact with a body that gave him a forceful shove, causing him to collide with a metal trash can. He somehow kept his balance and managed to hold on to the books in his arms. He spun around to find Joe Follson looming over him.

"Watch where you're going, Collie. You like messing with us, don't you? Well, you'll get yours. When Brock gets his chance, you're in for it."

David righted himself. He knew this was his opportunity to set his plan in motion. He spoke with confidence. "Shut up. You think I care what you guys have to say? I'm not scared of Brock. As a matter of fact, why don't you tell him that I'll meet him this Saturday. You idiots know the old water treatment plant, right? Three o'clock. You got that?"

Joe stood there dumbfounded. Then he smiled. "Are you serious, Collie? You really are that stupid, aren't you? You're making this too easy for us. Yeah, I'll tell him, and you better be there or else it's going to get done when you least expect it." Joe walked away shaking his head as other teens passed by, sneaking glances at David and whispering to one another.

David stood there, wide-eyed, hardly believing what he had just said to Joe. Not how I planned on getting Brock the word, but I guess it'll do. Wow, it was like I was a different person. He grinned and walked to his last class.

Back at home, David felt more alert than he had all day, but nausea started to set in. He still did not understand why he felt that way. Maybe it was just a lack of sleep like Mr. Worthing had said. He excused himself early from the dinner table with his mother. She noticed he had barely touched his food, but said nothing. He went upstairs, thankful to finally relax after his bizarre day and fell quickly asleep.

The sound of his mother shuffling about in her room awoke him. David stayed in his room and busied himself by going over his plans for this weekend again. He was not in the mood for his mother to trap him in conversation. The clock read 9:32, and David had pored over his blueprints for almost an hour. He started to feel anxiety as he contemplated his fate. The event was now only days away. He walked over to his closet and took out his shoebox, looking to decompress. He sat in his chair and opened the window to get some fresh air, then took the lid off the box.

After a half-hour, David stuck his head out into the cold night and took a couple of deep breaths. He listened to the nighttime noises as he peered out into the serene darkness of his backyard. David took in the tranquility of the moment as he stared at the moonlight reflected in the water pooled in a rectangular depression in the yard. A sandbox David's father constructed once sat in that area until it fell into disrepair. Steve ended up taking it down, which David resented even if he only used it as a child. The backyard held so many happy memories of his family, but the only activity it saw now was Steve practicing his golf game. Just one more reason to hate Steve.

David pulled his head back in the window and shut it. He packed up his shoebox and put it back in its place. The silence in the house told David that his mother had gone to sleep. Feeling hungry, he made his way down to the kitchen and opened the refrigerator looking for something appetizing. A noise at the back door startled David and froze him in his spot. He listened intently. It sounded like someone was trying to get in.

David quickly closed the refrigerator and stood with his back against it, out of view. His heart pounded. Whoever was trying to get in struggled with the door knob, twisting it back and forth. The sound of keys hitting cement eased David's fears as he realized it must be Steve trying to unlock the door since he did not come home right after work. The teen relaxed and tried to walk back upstairs unnoticed, but his stepfather managed to make his way inside before David could get out of the kitchen.

"Hey David." Steve spoke with impaired speech. "Where you headed?" David stopped, not sure if he should respond, having already had one confrontation today. "Are you going to answer me or just stand there like a fool?" David turned with a look of contempt. Over Steve's shoulder out the back window he could see that the car door had been left open. David could smell beer and a hint of fragrance.

He did not reply, and Steve took a step forward, intending to intimidate his stepson. "I wanna know the real reason you don't like me. Is it because I'm not your father?

Do you think I'm a bad person?" David stood silent. This, coming from a man who reeks of beer and perfume?

Steve raised his voice. "I try and try with you and get nothin' back. What's with you, kid?"

Beth's voice emanated from upstairs, but her words were indiscernible. Steve shot David a look of disgust as the teen quickly walked away, passing his mother on the stairs. She tried to stop him, but he slid by her. From his room, he could hear his mother argue with the drunkard in the kitchen. David smiled, knowing it would take a major miracle for Steve to get out of this latest screw-up. Maybe this will end in divorce if I'm lucky.

The arguing continued until David was not sure it would ever end. While he did feel empathy for his mother, she was the one who had created this mess by marrying Steve. David never understood how he could always see what a jerk Steve was, but his mother never could, at least not until recently. He never trusted Steve, even as a friend of his late father. David always got the feeling that Steve had ulterior motives, one being an interest in his mother.

The argument ended with Beth storming upstairs and Steve slamming the basement door. David could hear his mother sobbing in her room. He was half-tempted to go in and console her but decided against it. When his mother was hysterical like this, he usually chose to keep his distance, not knowing exactly what to say or do. After a while his mom quieted down and he heard her snoring. He laid down to get some sleep, for tomorrow was a day closer to his destiny.

CHAPTER 23

As David rode his bike down to the water plant, the sky filled with dark clouds. A storm was definitely blowing in. "How weird is this?" he muttered to himself. He got down to the field early enough that no one else was in sight. As he leaned his bike against the outside wall of the plant, a low rumbling filled the air, but it was not thunder. Something did not feel right. He glanced over his shoulder and saw more than a hundred kids advancing toward him, chanting for his demise.

"Let's get him!" one teen shouted. "Don't let him out of here alive!" another screamed.

This bloodthirsty cult of kids had come to see a fight and now they all seemed to want a piece of David. How did this happen?" The mob started charging toward him. David did not see Brock, Joe or Sean anywhere in the crowd. He panicked, not knowing where to turn, and then tried to make a run for the woods. He saw two figures off in the distance calling to him, waving him in to the safety of The Shadows. Dad? Sam? Is that them?

As he got closer, the two figures emerged from the woods; it was Sean and Joe. David quickly turned around and ran back toward the water plant, knowing it was the only shelter he could find at this point. The mob drew closer, shouting and cursing, some throwing rocks at David as he dashed to the plant. As his foot landed on the first step, the plant doors swung open. He stopped in his tracks. Brock stood in the entrance, looking more threatening than normal. David was now trapped between his nemesis and the mob. Brock rubbed his hands together and slammed the doors behind him with a thunderous bang. In an instant, everyone converged on David. He started screaming for his life as kids attacked him from all angles.

Beth ran into David's bedroom and turned on the light to witness her son thrashing around in his bed, yelling. She shook him vigorously. "David! David, it's okay. It's okay." David awoke and quickly sat up, and Beth backed off abruptly, not knowing how he would react. He sat there, panting and sweating, looking around the room.

"David, you were just having a night terror. Everything is fine."

David caught his breath before he spoke. "It just seemed so lifelike. I just didn't…"

"What, sweetheart? What were you dreaming about? Not the same as the one last month, was it?" His mom's question perplexed him. Last month? I don't remember that. He would just have to fake it – he knew he could not tell his mother what this night terror was really about.

"No, this was something different. It was all just such a blur. I'm okay now though. Thanks."

"All right, just try to get some sleep, and I'll see you in the morning." Beth closed the door and walked across the hallway to her room looking up at the ceiling in frustration.

David sat there confused, shaking his head. How does she know about some of the other nightmares I've had? I don't remember telling her about them. David glanced over at the clock glowing 12:53 a.m. That dream was enough to tell David that he was overly stressed about the weekend.

In the morning he dragged himself out of bed. Getting a shower, changing, and walking downstairs all took a major effort. David knew being this exhausted was not a good way to head into the weekend. The stage was now set for the fight, and he was sure word would spread significantly through school today. He likened high school whispers and gossip to an underground network. Only certain groups of people would know about the fight, and everyone would try their best to hide it from the administration. David did his best to avoid the chatter in the hallways and extra attention some people were giving him.

He labored through his classes trying his best to fight off the fatigue. Last thing he needed was any of his teachers getting on him for drifting off or falling asleep. With the rumors swirling about school David knew he already had enough eyes on him. If Brock, Sean or Joe were to mess with him today, he would not have the energy to defend himself.

145

He tried his best to ignore the stares and whispers as he walked the halls, but he noticed that even the jocks were acknowledging his presence. A couple of football players snickered at David and one mimicked punching an opponent as he passed. "That kid must be as crazy as he looks," he said to his buddies.

As he walked down the hall in between periods, David yawned, starting to feel a little tired again. Then adrenaline rushed through his body as he looked up to see Brock coming his way. David shifted one way and then another as he bumped into other students. "Watch it, man," one kid said as David stepped on his foot. Panic set in as Brock neared, although he seemed oblivious to David's close proximity. The distressed teen veered to his right, seeing the lavatory, and darted for it.

"Darn, someone's gotta go," one student remarked as David cut him off.

He hustled into a stall, locking it, and hung his book bag from the hook on the door. "Please, please, please, don't come in here," he whispered to himself.

He heard Brock's voice just outside. "Okay, yeah, I'll talk to you dudes later." David breathed a sigh of relief. It sounded like Brock was heading off to his next class. David put the toilet lid down, sitting on it and resting his head on his hands, when the bathroom door creaked open, startling him. He heard a melodic, playful whistle and footsteps walking over to the urinals. The person relieved himself and then went over to the sink. David grew impatient as he thought the student was taking his time. He heard a backpack unzipping while the faucet was still running and the sound of something being scrawled on a piece of paper. Next the person took several paper towels.

The water turned off and David began to feel anxious. In the reflection on the tile he saw the person approach his stall and stop in front of it. The figure made a quick movement. A clump of wet paper towels dropped on David's head and then fell to the floor. A moment later,

David saw a paper airplane slowly sail over the top of the stall as the figure walked out of the bathroom. The airplane swooped down, grazed his face, hit the side of the stall and then took a nosedive. David brushed it off as somebody just being a jerk. He grabbed his backpack off the hook and unlatched the lock. He looked down at the paper airplane and noticed writing on it. David picked it up and unfolded the loose-leaf paper. "YOU'RE DEAD" it read. He slumped back down on the toilet lid. It was Brock. He shook his head in despair, beginning to think his plan was not such a great idea.

David waited another couple of minutes just to be sure everyone was back in class, especially Brock. He concentrated on staying very mindful of his surroundings the rest of the school day. However, since word of the fight had made its way to many students' ears, it was difficult for him to keep a low profile. After school David sped down the street trying to make it to The Shadows as fast as possible so he could be home before his mother worried. He was eager to check on the layout of his traps since he had thought up some new ideas. Hopefully, Eugene had gotten around to digging out the pit a little more.

Riding across the field past the water plant, he glanced over at his makeshift barricade and knew he would have to make a few more tweaks to ensure it would hold up. The teen walked his bike down an incline, dropping it in some shrubs, and looked over his traps. He smiled as they all stood just as he had left them.

When he reached the spot where he wanted the pit, he had noticed that Eugene had made an attempt at digging it out, but had not gotten far. David gagged as the smell of vomit wafted up from the ditch Eugene had started. There was a small puddle of puke in the furrow. I guess I can't count on anyone else if I want this to work out right, he thought in frustration.

David searched for Eugene, but could not locate him. "Hey, Eugene, wherever you are…I have to go home, but I'll be back down tomorrow or Saturday. See you soon," the teen called out into the woods. He ran over to his bike and hurried home, since he could not risk spending any more time than he already had.

Eugene groaned. A voice awoke him, but did not know who it was. He rolled over in the dirt and squinted up at the canopy of the forest. He choked up some mucus and turned his head to spit it out. Then he rolled back on his stomach into the patch of overgrown weeds where he had passed out. Within seconds he was sleeping again.

CHAPTER 24

On Friday, David rode his bike to school through a slight drizzle. His mom had insisted on driving him, but he wanted to try and make it down to The Shadows after school if he could. He dreaded his meeting with Mr. Worthing today. *When are these meetings going to end? He has to realize that he's not getting anywhere with me and never will.* As David pulled up to the bike rack in the back of school, the drizzle subsided. He noticed several kids look his way as he locked up his bike and made his way inside. Walking down the hallway David heard much more chatter than in the past few days. *I guess this is to be expected. It's the day before.*

After his first few classes, David actually felt relieved to seek refuge in Mr. Worthing's office to get away from all the attention of other students. Heading into another session did not please David, but he was hoping both the meetings and unwanted spotlight on him would end soon. He walked into the office without saying a word and shut the door behind him with a bang.

"Well, that's not a good start. What's up, David?"

The teen shrugged his shoulders. "Bad day."

Mr. Worthing took a deep breath through his nose and studied his subject. "All right. Well, how about you just stay here while I go get some cups and ice. I've got some more sodas for us. Okay?"

David sat slumped in the chair and just nodded his head. Mr. Worthing walked out and shut the door behind him, leaving David alone with his thoughts.

The teen's mind raced from the counseling sessions to what would occur tomorrow at the fight. He shook his head as his anxiety surged. Within the past few weeks he had found himself at the center of attention of the student body and the guidance counselor. At home his mother was more involved with him than she had been in years, and he was at drastic odds with his stepfather. How did things get so out of control?

As he leaned his head back, the door swung open, startling him. The guidance counselor walked in balancing two cups of ice in one hand as he shut the door with the other. As he placed the cups on his desk, one cup slipped out of his hand. The bottom of the cup hit the desk, causing a mist to emanate from the top. Mr. Worthing quickly righted the cup and poured each of them a soda. He offered one to the student. David grabbed his cup and took a couple of gulps as the guidance counselor took his seat.

"So, what's up, David? What's wrong?"

David shook his head, looking around the room to avoid eye contact. His crunched on a piece of ice, spitting shards of it back into the cup. "Nothing, just school. You know by now I don't like school."

Mr. Worthing tilted his head back and looked at the ceiling. "You don't have to, David. I'm not here to tell you what to like and not to like. I'm just here to listen, really."

David took another drink of the soda to finish it off, then continued to chew on the ice. "Well, then what am I here for? What is all of this? We've gotten nowhere."

Mr. Worthing took a sip of his soda and paused before he answered. "It is what you make it."

The teen sat there perplexed. "What does that even mean?"

The man did not answer the sarcastic question. They sat in silence for a minute as Mr. Worthing wanted to give David time to gather his thoughts. David yawned and his eyes started to blink as he slouched back in the chair. The counselor looked up at the clock. "You know what, David, how about I give you a few minutes to yourself?"

As he left the room, he failed to shut the door all the way and it creaked open a couple of inches. The overconfident guidance counselor walked down the hallway into the bathroom, content with the course of action he had taken during the last two meetings. He bent down to look

150

under the stalls to check that no one else was in the room, then looked at himself in the mirror. "It's all going to work out fine," he said aloud. He walked into the end stall and checked his watch.

Back in the counselor's office, David found himself feeling groggy. His head bobbed as he fought to stay awake, but within a few seconds he gave in. His eyes closed and his body went limp in the chair.

A moment later, Mr. Mitchell walked by and glanced in the open door. He saw the teen asleep in the chair by himself. What the hell? He pushed the door open with urgency and hovered over David, not sure what to do. He was anticipating the boy would feel his presence and wake on his own. "What is going on here?" he muttered to himself.

Meanwhile, Tyler Worthing washed his hands, left the bathroom and strolled back down the hall. He checked his watch to see that ten minutes had passed. As he approached his office and saw the door wide open, he thought David had left again. As he walked into his office, he found the principal reclining the chair for the unconscious student.

"Mr. Mitchell...I...I..." The counselor struggled to put a sentence together, stumbling over his words.

The principal turned, eyes wide in anger, as he spoke through clenched teeth. "Outside now, Mr. Worthing."

The two men walked out into the hall, shutting the door behind them. "What in the hell is going on here, Tyler? You'd better have a good explanation for this after last week's screw-up."

Tyler wore an astonished look on his face.

"Oh, you didn't think I knew, did you?"

The counselor shuffled his feet. "Sir, I will handle it. I promise you. We are making good progress, and I have the audio to support that. I'm telling you, sir, I've got this."

The principal ran his hand through his hair, pacing. "You've got this? You have the door open with a student who looks half dead sitting in your office by himself. What are you doing?"

The counselor had sustained the principal's demeaning attitude long enough. "I'm doing what you told me to do, sir – whatever is necessary to get results. You think this kid is a potential threat, and I'm going to find out if that's true. Let me do my job, and I will get you what you need."

The counselor's vehement response shocked Roy Mitchell as no one at the school ever talked to him in such a manner. He took a step forward and stared into the counselor's eyes. "You'd better get me results." He strode off down the hall. Tyler Worthing reentered his office, shaking his head, and locked the door behind him.

Mr. Gavin stepped out from an adjoining breezeway. Judging by the brief conversation he had overheard, he knew something was not right. The hall monitor approached the counselor's door and put his ear to it.

CHAPTER 25

After the counselor moved David over to the recliner he grabbed his tape recorder and other materials from his desk. He took a deep breath and pulled up a chair next to David, positioning the recorder on the other chair next to the teen. The counselor repeated the steps that had been successful at the last session until he elicited a response. He started with exploratory questions, beginning with the death of David's father and brother. The boy muttered, twitching in his hypnotic trance, reliving the moments of that trauma and the guilt he felt.

Outside the door, John Gavin shook his head, appalled by what he was hearing, and walked away. The hall monitor did not know what course of action he could take knowing that Roy Mitchell was ultimately behind this debacle. He thought about what he could do, if anything, without backlash from the conniving principal. If anything happens to this kid, I know where to look.

In the office, the counselor was taking notes as he steered the teen's subconscious to his current personal life. David spoke about his hatred of his stepfather and his growing annoyance with his meddling mother. Fifteen minutes into the therapy session David began expounding on his present state of affairs at school. Dislike of homework, some teachers and various students dominated his thoughts.

Tyler Worthing's eyes grew wide as the teen murmured about his several run-ins with Brock and his group. The counselor rubbed his hands together. Here we go. This is what I've been waiting for. The session was especially surreal as it seemed he was finally able to release his subject's true feelings and secrets.

David trailed off, then began mumbling about a plan for the weekend. His speech became garbled and the counselor could make sense of only a few phrases. Making traps? What's that about? He did not put much stock in what he was hearing – he was most interested in the teen's general feelings, not his weekend plans in the woods. A few names came up and the counselor jotted them down to see if he could make any school connections.

The teen shifted to talking about his friend Aaron and their periodic phone conversations. He mentioned Luke and their recent nighttime journey to vandalize Brock's house. The counselor underlined that in his notes – he had heard about that incident.

Next, David rambled on about The Shadows and how he liked to wander around there to get away from the pressures of his everyday life. He talked about hanging out with Patrick and Eugene down there, which astounded the counselor. He found it hard to believe this loner had so many friends inside or outside of school. It didn't add up.

Time was about to run out on the session, but David kept on murmuring, still in a hypnotic trance. The counselor's hand began to cramp from taking notes, struggling to keep up with the boy's continuous dialogue. The period bell rang and students filled the hallways, but David did not react to the sound of the bell.

Down the hall, Mr. Mitchell walked toward the guidance counselor's office amidst the chaos of students flocking to their next classes. He had a strong feeling, from speaking with the counselor and what his own eyes saw, that things were not going as planned. Maybe it's time to pull the plug on this experiment, he thought.

He approached the door and hesitated before he gave a quick knock and twisted the doorknob. Locked. He jiggled the knob a few times and knocked again. "Mr. Worthing, are you in there?"

Tyler leapt up from his chair in a panic. He quickly unlocked the door, opened it a crack and whispered to the principal, "I'm kind of busy, Mr. Mitchell."

The principal tried to look over the counselor's shoulder. "What's going on in there? Your session should have ended already. This boy needs to get to class." Tyler

Worthing glanced back at David and then looked at the principal, not knowing what to say.

The principal glared at him intensely. "I'm warning you, Tyler! What is going on in here? Don't make me..."

Tyler Worthing cut him off, opening the door and gesturing him inside. "Okay, sir, okay. You may have to see this for yourself to understand it." The principal could not believe the scene before him. An apparently unconscious David Collie sprawled in the recliner, murmuring incoherently.

"What is the meaning of this?"

"Sir, you said take whatever means I thought necessary to get into this boy's mind."

The principal rubbed his temples. "This is bad, this is real bad."

Tyler Worthing looked over at the teen. "He's just hypnotized. He'll be fine, and he won't remember a thing."

The principal was incredulous. "Have you lost your mind? How did you even get him under hypnosis? Teachers can barely get him to do his homework, let alone something to this extent."

The guidance counselor swallowed hard. "I've been studying up on hypnosis. I gave him a little bit of a sleeping agent. He should have only been out for about a half-hour, but he must be very comfortable. The book said in some cases subjects can go a little while longer if they reach the threshold of REM sleep."

Mr. Mitchell rubbed his head again and turned, his eyes bulging. "Sleeping agent? A book? Do you even know what the hell you are doing? This is crazy. Do you know I have been hearing reports of this kid having full-blown conversations with himself here at school? Whatever you're doing is probably screwing him up even more."

Tyler looked at the principal with anger and frustration. "This was your idea, sir, your idea. You're the one who wanted to start this experiment. You're the one who wanted to identify potential threats to the school. You yourself said this was going to be some kind of revolutionary new program that could be adopted by schools nationwide. I have been under so much pressure from you to produce results that I resorted to extreme measures, but I assure you this is not harming him."

The principal turned nearly purple with rage, and the counselor knew he had gone too far. But before Mr. Mitchell could say anything further, David began to stir, prompting both men to step into the hallway. Mr. Mitchell calmed himself before he spoke. "Tyler, I believe that kids like David are one day gonna explode and resort to something extreme to get back at the kids who bully them. That's what you are supposed to be examining with David, not experimenting with voodoo. I thought you were an accomplished guidance counselor. Yes, this was my idea, but you're the one who chose to go this route, not me. We were supposed to make a determination from your findings and go on from there."

"Well, that's what I…"

"And another thing. If you ever speak to me that way again, I will have your butt out of here so fast it will make your head spin. And I guarantee that you will never work in a school again."

Back in the office David was droning on about his hatred of Brock and his detailed plans for revenge on Saturday. He spoke of how he despised other kids at school and the potential consequences for them as well. Unbeknownst to Tyler Worthing, the dark secrets that David had been holding back were all coming out, alas for no one to hear.

The tape recorder button popped up as the cassette was full. The sound snapped David out of his trance. He looked around the room, taking a few seconds to realize where he was. When his eyes focused again, he could see the profiles of two men through the frosted glass of the office door. He knew one had to be Mr. Worthing, then he recognized the muffled voice of the other as Principal

Mitchell. He could not make out what they were saying, but figured it had to be about him.

David looked over at the recorder not comprehending at first why it was sitting next to him. He then saw the hypnosis book lying on the desk and started to understand what might have transpired during these most recent sessions. He looked at the empty cup he had used earlier. So that's why I've been falling asleep in here. He pushed the eject button on the recorder, grabbed the tape, and quickly shut the cassette deck. He put the cassette in his pocket and leaned forward, trying to hear the conversation outside the door.

After a couple of minutes it was apparent that the men had come to some sort of an agreement. David lay back down, acting like he was still under hypnosis as he heard the door open slightly.

"Okay, Mr. Mitchell, I'll be by in about fifteen minutes," Tyler Worthing said. The guidance counselor noticed that David was no longer rambling, which meant he would probably awaken soon. David decided to move a bit to distract Mr. Worthing from realizing the tape was missing. The diversion was successful as the counselor rushed to put all of his materials back into the desk drawer.

Tyler Worthing sat back down in his chair and acted preoccupied by reading the newspaper. David blinked and sat up. "Mr. Worthing, what happened?"

The counselor put the paper down and acted surprised that David was awake. "David, finally. I was beginning to worry. You fell asleep again. I had to bring the nurse in again for precautionary measures, but I might have to speak to your mom about this. She may want you to see a doctor about this lethargy. You might have mono or something."

Perceiving what he did now, David was well aware the counselor had no other recourse or action. The teen also knew Mr. Worthing had no idea he had unraveled the entire farce behind the sessions. "I don't know why that keeps happening, but I feel fine." David looked up at the clock. "I'm late for my next class." Mr. Worthing reached into his desk, grabbed a late pass and handed it to David. "Thanks," David said. He walked out of the office smiling, knowing he had all the evidence he would need to take those two down in due time. They just messed with the wrong kid, he thought and patted the tape in his pocket.

Back in his office the guidance counselor took a deep breath and gathered himself to go see his boss. Tyler Worthing knew he had to meet with Mrs. Mathis and tell her what he thought she should know, regardless of what Principal Mitchell wanted. He knew he had a troubled boy on his hands whose mother needed to get him professional help. The counselor had concerns about David, but from what he had heard did not think he was a threat to the school or other students. Unfortunately, he had not heard the truly disturbing things David had said about Brock and the students on whom he wanted to exact retribution.

In his meeting with the principal, the counselor was much calmer than he had been a twenty minutes earlier. Both men agreed that they had to work together to deal with this situation the correct way even though they both had their own private agendas. Mitchell acknowledged that David's mother should come in, but he wanted to be part of that conversation. "Tyler, this whole pilot program was initiated in order to feel out troubled students. I wanted to be able to develop a system to get a solid understanding of how their minds work. That's where you came in, but after that stunt you pulled in there, I have my reservations. Then I got to thinking – if your technique does show results and we can stop a student like David from doing something rash, this could work. I'm telling you, school violence is going to become all too commonplace one day, and we could be the ones to help prevent some of it."

To hear this change of opinion from Mr. Mitchell in such a short period of time disillusioned Tyler. However, he knew the man before him was more interested in the recognition and money this could bring him than actually helping students. The counselor knew he had more of a conscience than his egotistical employer even if he had drugged a student into hypnosis. Tyler knew he had done it with the good intention of helping David and his mother. I have to find a way to sort this mess out on my terms, he thought as he walked out of the principal's office.

CHAPTER 26

After leaving the guidance counselor's office, David had no intention of going directly to his next class. With his late pass he figured he could wait it out in the back room of the gym and relax. He fell onto the mats and nearly dozed off, but was kept awake by the bouncing of basketballs in the adjoining main gym. I hate gym class, he thought. Once there was silence, he knew that the kids had gone to the locker room and that it would not be long before the period bell rang. After the extended rest, he felt a little better. On his way out of the gym, he almost bumped into a girl who seemed to come out of nowhere. "Sorry," he said as he passed by her.

"Wait," the girl called out. She caught up to him. "You're David Collie, right?"

David looked puzzled. A girl, talking to me? He gave her a suspicious look. "Uh, yeah."

"Thought so. I've been meaning to talk to you. There's a buzz going around school that something is going down tomorrow between you and Brock Shills. I would like to help you if I could." David turned to walk away without responding. He did not need any more exposure of his plan. "Hold on! Please, let me explain. I should have started with this. You see, Brock and those other jerks picked on my brother so bad last year that my mom almost had him change schools. I would love to see those guys get what's coming to them."

David began to feel a little dizzy again, like after his last counseling session, but now knew the actual cause. Down the hall, John Gavin looked at David, then up at the white drop-ceiling and took a breath. I'm leaving this one alone, the weathered hall monitor thought to himself as he walked around the corner to the other wing.

David scratched the back of his neck. "If you put it that way, then sure, I guess. Tell you what, a couple of us are meeting down by the water treatment plant around noon. Come on down, if you want in."

"Great, thanks." She smiled and started walking away. David started in the opposite direction when he realized that in his fog he never asked the girl's name, let alone who her brother was. He turned. "What's your…" His voice trailed off. The girl was nowhere in sight.

At the end of the day, Luke approached David at his locker. "Hey, David. What's up, man?" David went about his business, trying to ignore the kid standing next to him. Luke brushed off David's neglect and kept talking. "I know it's been a while, but I heard about tomorrow and I…" Before he could get out another word, David slammed his locker shut, drawing some stares from nearby students.

"Shut up for a second," David said angrily. He grabbed Luke's arm and ushered him into the bathroom. They walked to the back of the lavatory as David paced in an attempt to calm down. A kid came out of a stall and looked over at David curiously as he quickly washed his hands and left. "First off, you smash Brock's window and leave me sitting there? His dad almost ran me down! Now you show up out of nowhere and think everything between us is fine? You're nuts, kid!"

"Okay, okay. I screwed up, but I hate Brock. I didn't expect you to freeze up. I assumed you were right behind me. When I looked back and didn't see you, I thought you just took off a different way." David shook his head, refusing to believe his story and strode towards the door. Luke stepped in David's path, stopping him. "David, I want to do this thing with you tomorrow. My sister Kelly just told me that she spoke to you about helping out. You know those guys picked on me just as bad as you? It was crappy, real crappy. Please, can I help?"

David's anger began to subside as Luke seemed sincere. "That was your sister? She was gone before I could find out who she was."

161

"Yeah, she likes to look out for me. She went to you on her own. I had nothing to do with that."

Now that David had confronted Luke about his betrayal, he felt he could trust the kid. "All right, Luke. You can come. A few of us, including your sister, are meeting down by the treatment plant at noon. No more surprises, though. This time you follow my lead. Got it?"

Luke nodded. "Got it. See you there."

The last of the remaining students were hustling to get out of school, leaving the hallways desolate. On his way out, David stopped to look at a bulletin board with the headline "1986: Year in Rewind." The board displayed photographs of the school's sports, clubs and students at various times throughout the year. There were also newspaper and magazine articles along with pop culture references. He looked them over cynically, snickering to himself at the emotional attachment people had to this collage.

"'Scuse me, dude." David moved out of the way and watched as a kid pinned a newspaper clipping to the board. He saw it was an article about the Challenger explosion from earlier in the year and stood there reading it as the other student backed away. "That was horrible, wasn't it?" David just nodded as he kept on reading. "We finally decided it was time to put it up here. A lot of people had a tough time with this one," the student said.

"Yeah. Sometimes things happen people aren't ready for."

"You got that right, man. Well, take it easy."

David glanced at the kid walking down the hall, taking notice of his stonewashed jeans and ironed collared shirt. Look at that kid. I have nothing in common with him, just like most everyone else at this school. At least he didn't know who I was. David removed the Challenger article from the board and put it in his backpack. Then he took a step back and spit on the display in disgust. He exited the school as the spittle slowly ran down the collage.

162

Outside David slung his backpack over his shoulders and unlocked his bike. He took a long look around and thought for a minute. The rain started to come down, telling David there was no chance he could make it to The Shadows. Mom would be too worried. That's the last thing I need, he thought as he pedaled away.

In the back parking lot of the school, Brock, Sean and Joe sat in Brad Silver's car watching David. "You want to mess with him?" asked Brad.

"Nah, he's getting his tomorrow, big time. Just ride by him real slow," Brock said.   As David coasted down the school's exit roadway, the IROC-Z rolled by with its heavy customized engine rumbling. All of the boys in the car stared at David as they passed by slowly, a mere twenty feet away.

David stopped his bike and glared back unflinching as the precipitation landed on his face. Brock smirked at him as they turned onto the street. Sean stuck his head out the window yelling, "Woo-hoo!" as Brad stepped on the gas. The tires screeched and smoked as the car sped away.

CHAPTER 27

In his office, Tyler Worthing was packing up his things to go home for the weekend. He put away a couple of files and then unlocked his drawer to grab the cassette tape containing the audio of David's session. He placed the recorder on his desk and pushed the eject button. Anxiety rushed over his body when he saw the cassette deck was empty. *What did I do with it?* He got on his hands and knees and looked under his desk, surveying the entire floor. He checked in his drawers and scanned his desk. He sat down in his chair, wondering what could have happened to the tape. *It couldn't have been Mitchell. I just came back from his office, and the door was locked while I was gone. Who else could have been in here?*

After a few minutes of thinking, a notion struck him. *David. I thought he left here in a more unusual mood than normal. He must have woken up before I came back in and figured out what was going on.* The guidance counselor rested his face in his hands, not knowing how to rectify the situation. He knew that if the tape got out, he could lose his job and possibly go to jail should David and his family choose to go that route. *Think, dummy, think.* He picked up a pencil and tapped it on the desk, mulling over the very few options he had. *I have to call his mother and try to explain things to her. That's the only way to stop this from spinning out of my control.*

Mr. Worthing opened David's file and located his home phone number. He dialed the number and waited for an answer as he concentrated on trying to keep the panic out of his voice. After the fourth ring, he heard Beth Mathis' voice on the other end.

"Hello?"

"Mrs. Mathis, this is Tyler Worthing, the guidance counselor from David's school."

Beth smiled on the other end of the line. She had become fond of Tyler after meeting him. "Oh, yes, Tyler, how are you? Is everything okay?"

He tried to speak calmly. "Ah, yes, everything is fine. I wanted to see if you could meet me at my office tomorrow. I just want to discuss some things about David that have come up recently. If it's a bad time, I understand. I know Saturday meetings are a little unorthodox, but I'm pretty booked up next week."

Beth eyes grew wide. "Well, if you think it's that important, I can stop by when I'm out running my errands. What time were you thinking? Are you sure everything is okay?"

"Yes, it's not an emergency or anything like that. I just want to catch you up on our progress. How does two o'clock sound?"

Beth bit her lip and thought, putting her hand to her forehead. "Um, yes, that's fine. See you then."

Tyler could hear the concern in her voice. "Okay great, see you tomorrow then. Bye." He sat back in his chair, admitting to himself that he was desperate to speak with her before David told her anything. He could tell that she knew something was not right. That kid is much smarter than he lets on. He could have been faking these sessions the entire time. Tyler sat for a while trying to think of a way he could come clean to Mrs. Mathis about the counseling appointments. The only positive was being able to sneak in this meeting with David's mother on the weekend unbeknownst to the principal.

On his way home, David had to seek shelter under a tree as the rain had really started to come down. With the thunder rumbling overhead, he began to consider all the challenges he was currently up against. Not only would he come face to face with his adversary tomorrow, but he also had to coordinate a group of misfits to help him carry out his plan.

Only a couple hours earlier he had uncovered a plot by the guidance counselor and principal to use him as some sort of test subject for their experiment. It seemed that the majority of students were becoming fixated on David and the rumors that surrounded him. Even something as innocent as a walk down the hallway brought stares from other students. David was hoping tomorrow would bring him some kind of closure.

David arrived home wet from the storm, but his mother did not hassle him. She tried to stay calm in the wake of the phone call she had just received. After dinner with his mother, with Steve still relegated to the basement, David excused himself and went upstairs. He knew that the next time he saw his mother it might be from a hospital bed if Brock got hold of him tomorrow.

Up in his room he envisioned the ideal scenario of how the encounter would unfold the following day. Brock comes down to the old treatment plant. We'll have words until he's so pissed that he can't take it anymore. When he tries to come after me through the barricade, I make a run for it. He mentally ran through the exact path he would take that would guide the action into the booby-trapped woods. David envisioned it over again and again, trying to cover all the different contingencies, until he felt confident in his final plan.

He reached over, grabbed his phone and punched in a number. After a few seconds, he heard Aaron's voice on the other end. The two discussed the next day's setup, and Aaron agreed to meet him early to help get everything in order. After the phone call, David set the phone on the floor next to his bed and went over his drawings a few more times, making some minor adjustments.

As the night wore on, the nervous feeling in his stomach got worse as he knew that each passing second drew him closer to the big event. Lying back on his bed, David felt something poke him. The tape. I almost forgot about this, but I know what to do with it. He went into the closet and pulled out his shoebox, sifting through it and looking over the contents. He put the cassette tape inside, laid a note over top of it, and put the box back in the hidden compartment. David needed to use Steve's stereo in the basement to listen to it and now was not the time.

If David's scheme were to backfire tomorrow, he wanted to make sure other people had what was coming to them. If something were to happen to him, he knew his mom would go looking through his room, like she did in Sam's room after his death, and find the shoebox with the tape. I know it won't come to the worst possible scenario, but you never can be too sure, he thought.

That night David did not have any trouble falling asleep. He was mentally and physically drained, but he was also finally at peace with what was ahead of him. He got the best night's sleep he had had in a long time.

On Saturday, David woke up at nine o'clock and felt refreshed. He looked out his bedroom window to see the sun shining and got the sense that it was going to be a good day. Then he made a checklist of the things he needed done at The Shadows to make sure he had everything covered. He went downstairs and ate some cereal by himself at the kitchen table until his mom walked into the kitchen.

"Good morning. You're up early," she said as she walked over to make a pot of coffee.

"I know. I just didn't feel like sleeping in. Figured I would come down to talk to you."

Her son's response stunned her. This is something new, she thought. She poured a mug of coffee and sat down with her son. "What are you up to today?"

"I'm going to head out in a bit to meet up with some other kids."

Beth had to hold back from spitting out her coffee in amazement. She did not want to seem overly curious because it could cause her son to shut her out. She just wanted to be happy for him. "That's great, honey. Who are these people and what are you guys up to?"

David had prepared himself for a possible interrogation. "Just a couple guys I know. Probably gonna ride around. Nothing big."

Beth did not know what to make of it. She had never known her son to hang around with anyone until recently, let alone a group of other boys. Maybe these sessions with Mr. Worthing are finally getting through to him, she thought. Beth decided to stop her questioning there, not wanting to pry too much since this was a big step forward for David.

"Where's he going to be today?" David asked, nodding his head towards the basement.

Beth was curious that David was even the slightest bit concerned with what Steve was doing. "Well, after what happened lately between the two of you, he knows going out to golf or doing whatever he wants isn't his best option right now. He has to fix a few things around the house and do some touch-up painting, which I have been asking him to do forever. Why do you ask?"

David swallowed the last of the cereal, delaying his response. "No reason. Just wondering." He brought the cereal bowl to his lips and drank the remainder of the milk, then excused himself to go upstairs and get ready. Before he turned the corner into the living room, David looked back at his mother. "Sorry if I have been a pain lately, Mom. I just have a lot of things on my mind."

His mother's eyes got glassy as she fought back tears. "You don't have to apologize for anything, David. Just go outside and have some fun." After she heard his bedroom door shut, Beth put her head down on her arms and started to sob. She felt sorrow for the hurt her son had endured and happiness that he might be getting better. She had not seen this kind of encouraging behavior in David in a long time. Maybe the meeting with Mr. Worthing would not be to hear what she had feared.

Down in the basement, Steve had been listening in and managed to make out most of the conversation. David was playing on his mother's emotions yet again and it frustrated Steve. He had to figure out a way to get back in his wife's good graces soon. This kid could ruin my entire marriage. He's definitely acting peculiar, Steve thought.

Upstairs in the shower, David realized today would be a defining moment in his life. Maybe this will change things for me for the better. I have to believe everything will turn out okay.

The teen changed and readied his backpack, which contained his notepad, drawings, and a change of clothes, just in case. He attached a watch to his bag, as he had to keep track of the time so it would all go down as planned. He threw the backpack over his shoulder and ran down the steps. It was closing in on 10:30.

"All right, Mom, I'll see you later," he said as he walked by her in the kitchen.

Before he could make it to the door, she stopped him. "Wait a minute."

What is it now? Does she know something? he thought.

"I packed you a snack." His mom handed him a brown paper bag. "I'll be out running errands later on this afternoon, just to let you know," she said.

"Right. Thanks, Mom." He snatched the brown paper bag out of her hand and grabbed the plastic sports bottle filled with water off the counter.

Beth watched him leave the house, grab his bike out of the garage and glided down the driveway. It was strange that her son was in such an upbeat mood, but she figured he was just excited to hang out with other kids for a change. He hasn't brought a friend over here since the accident. Hopefully that changes soon, and it sounds like it just may.

169

David rode through his neighborhood not knowing what would become of his life in the next few hours. He saw a couple of neighbors doing yard work on the sunny morning. One man was washing his car with a bucket full of suds and a sponge. An older woman sitting on her porch in a smock gave David a wave as he went by. Looking at his neighborhood in admiration as he coasted down the street gave him a confidence boost, as if these people were pulling for him. A positive feeling swept over him as he smiled and pedaled faster, speeding away.

When he reached the water plant access road, David stopped and thought about the situation he was about to get into. He saw that the "For Sale" sign was still down. David figured that the people selling this property cared so little about it that they hadn't replaced the sign or even checked up on it for that matter. The teen took a deep breath and walked his bike through the expansive vacant field that led to the lifeless plant.

Hopping back on his bike, David rode around the obstructions that he set in place for a quick drive-by inspection. He continued on towards the woods and stopped his bike at the edge of The Shadows. He looked down through the brush and could see Patrick and Eugene were already at work prepping the area.

David sat there on his bike for a minute and watched as the two labored. I can't believe I actually have people willing to help me when most people just turn their backs on me. What makes these guys different? Knowing he could not waste any more time, David called down to Patrick and Eugene, motioning for them to come up to the field. Patrick made his way up the incline, but the homeless man stayed back, taking a rest on a tree stump.

"How's it going?" Patrick asked.

David stared down at Eugene shaking his head. "What's his problem?"

Patrick patted him on the shoulder. "Don't worry about him. He's just tired. Eugene has been at it all morning. So why are we up here?"

David turned his bike and walked it in the direction of the water treatment plant, surprised to hear how hard Eugene had been working on his behalf. "Some other people are coming down to help and should be here in a little while. A couple kids from school and my friend Aaron are meeting us by the plant. I wanted to run through the beginning stages of this plan." When they got to the water plant steps, David leaned his bike against the railing and pointed out the objects that would serve as his barricade.

"Are you sure this is going to work, man?" Patrick asked with concern in his voice.

David pretended not to hear his friend's question, not wanting to start second guessing himself this close to the fight. He walked around the structure not saying a word and trying to look busy. Patrick sensed that he might have offended David and made some suggestions. The two of them moved parts of the blockade until the most practical set-up satisfied them.

They walked over to sit on the steps of the plant, exchanging ideas and scenarios of what was to take place in a few hours. David got the feeling Patrick didn't have a lot of confidence in his plan. Anxiety began to wash over him. Then, in the distance, David saw a few figures walk onto the field. Luke, his sister Kelly, and Aaron strolled toward them.

"Here they come now. They must have run into each other on the way here," David said, standing up.

Patrick turned his head to look. "Who?"

David glared at his friend in annoyance. "The other kids coming to help us. I just told you about them. That kid is Luke, that's his sister, and Aaron is in the back." Patrick looked confused and stayed seated as David pointed them out. "Hey, guys, this is Patrick. He knows these woods just about as good as me. Now listen up. Here's how I want it to play out." No one had any questions as they watched David run through the motions of his scenario. Then a thought crossed Patrick's mind.

"How are you going to get them to chase you if you are supposed to fight Brock up here in the field?" To answer his question David walked over to a large truck tire that was part of the makeshift barrier. He reached inside and pulled out the metal pipe he had planted there earlier.

"With this," he said, as he held it up for them all to see. "In order for them to chase me they have to be pissed, right? Well, if getting wise with Brock doesn't work, then I'll just have to use this to get things going." Everyone seemed to agree with David's thinking, as he apparently had every aspect covered.

They all followed him to the edge of the woods and down the loose dirt hill that led to his series of traps. "Okay, everyone, this is where those guys get their payback. Since Sean and Joe are Brock's puppets, and supposing that they are both faster than that lard Brock, they'll probably be after me first. Watching Brock pummel me up on that field is what most of the crowd will want to see. Brock seeks nothing more than to humiliate me in front of everyone. But I hope to get my revenge today, and I know you are all here to help me do that." David looked around at everyone. Patrick wore a contemptuous look on his face.

"What's wrong?" David asked him.

Patrick snapped out of his daze. "Oh, nothing. Yeah, sounds good to me." David started to wonder if Patrick doubted the proposed execution of his plan.

"Okay, everyone, let's pick up rocks or anything with some weight to it that can be easily thrown. I want Luke, Kelly and Aaron stationed up on these rises on either side of the path after you see them coming. You guys can shower them with rocks and whatever else you find to distract them from noticing the traps as they chase me," David said. Patrick began to collect rocks from the side of the path as David walked away to see Eugene. He spoke for

172

a few minutes with Eugene, who brought him up to speed on what he had accomplished. David called out for everyone to gather around. Eugene and Patrick exchanged glances and nodded.

David walked down the path to the small pile of rocks, sticks and some hard green pods that fell from some nearby trees. "Guys, this is it? We need to find more later, but for now take these up to wherever you want to station yourselves."

Patrick gathered up the pile. "Don't worry, David, I'll help these guys. You can get started on the traps." David pulled out the blueprints from his backpack and looked them over while walking over to the set of trees that marked the start of the ambush. By the time he finished assessing the area, Patrick and the others had returned, while Eugene was still filling the mud pit.

"Okay, we're gonna set the first one here. I'm going to tie a fishing line around each tree trunk to make a tripwire across the path. I already gathered some jagged rocks and thorny brush to put on the ground just after the tripwire. Whoever takes the fall on this one will most likely get pretty torn up," David said. No one seemed to be against the plan despite how brutal it sounded. "We're going to need some more rocks and prickly brush for this and then cover it with leaves so they don't see it."

"I'm on it," Patrick blurted out and began searching around. David worked on tying the fishing line around the trees and spread out the rocks and brush on the ground as Patrick came back with more.

David glanced around and saw the others were gone. "It's about time they started doing something. It might have been a mistake telling them about this. They could blow this whole thing, especially Luke and his sister," he said tensely.

Patrick looked around, thinking of something to say to calm David down. "They are probably just nervous and don't know what to do. I'll stay on them, so just do what you got to do."

After David completed the initial booby trap, and got everyone together again, he led the group down the path to the second set of trees. He pulled out his plans. "This is the spot for the next one. We're going to dig a series of holes like this." He outlined several circles on the ground with a stick. "They should cover this area as wide as the path and a stretch out about ten feet. Then we can cover this trap with leaves as well."

David noticed the fretful look on a few faces and felt he needed to explain. "I need these traps to be foolproof or else I'll be in trouble, which is why they may seem a little severe. If you don't want to be a part of this you can leave, but I'm doing this for me and any other kid that has been picked on by one of these pieces of garbage. After all, they'll survive this. I know I will."

Patrick patted David on the back. "Why don't you get started on these holes while I take these guys over to meet Eugene? I'll come back and help you finish it up. You gotta relax a little, man. We're behind you on this, okay?"

David nodded. He watched in frustration as Patrick walked away with Luke, Kelly, and Aaron. What's Patrick trying to do here? Could there be any way that he's trying to sabotage me for some reason? I'll have to double-check everything after he's done, David thought. While the others were off getting acquainted with Eugene, David took his frustration out on digging the holes.

When he had about half the holes dug out, he needed a rest. I have to be careful not to tire myself out before this whole thing even starts. He sat down on a large rock. Eugene continued the tedious task of filling the pit with river mud via the bucket as Patrick and the others walked up to David.

"You want us to finish this while you go do something else? I know you have a lot on your mind and want to have enough energy for later," Luke said.

"Thanks, Luke. If you don't mind taking it from here I would appreciate that."

Patrick stepped forward and took hold of the shovel. "I'll handle this, David."

David stood up and looked at Patrick sternly. "Make sure you dig them like the others I did. We have to have everything as close to perfect as possible." The disgruntled teen walked off as Patrick glared after at him. What's his problem? he thought.

David turned around and snapped, "Come on, guys. The rest of you can take a look at these other traps."

David came upon Eugene who was getting close to completely filling up the pit.

"What's up, Eugene? Coming along pretty good, I see. You met all those guys, right?"

Eugene stopped for a minute and wiped his brow. "Coming along real well, David. Yeah, I did meet your friends. Let me ask you something. Are you sure you're ready for this? These surveyors we're dealing with here are grown men who are probably stronger than both of us combined."

David hesitated, trying to keep his story straight. If Eugene knew these traps were set for high school kids, he would most likely put a stop to the whole thing. "I'm sure about this, Eugene. No one is taking these woods from us. I really appreciate the help."

David moved on to his next set-up as Eugene got back to work. "Remember to top it off with leaves when you're done filling it," David called back. The homeless man waved as he walked back towards the river with the filthy bucket.

While making his way up the rise by Eugene's campsite, he surveyed the area, getting a feel for the trajectory of his final device. He got to the top and waited for Eugene to pour more muck into the pit and go back to the riverbank so he was out of the way. David gave the splintered stump a vigorous side toss and watched as it swung down and skidded against the ground, coming to a stop just before the pit.

After he made some adjustments to the slack of the rope, he reset the stump at the top of the rise. David gave it another heave and watched as it forcefully swung back and forth like a pendulum over the pit.

He went back down, retrieved the stump, and carried it back up to the spot in order to continue the exercise until he got a feel for it. David would have to get Eugene to make sure Brock did not go any farther if he made it to the mud pit. If it comes to this, Eugene is going to be really confused as to why a high school kid is chasing me, David thought. I just gotta hope he can stall him here somehow.

Eugene stood off to the side staying out of the way of the stump and just watched David, shaking his head. Patrick sidled up to Eugene. He had just finished digging the last series of holes. "That kid is crazy, isn't he?" Eugene said.

"You should ask his friends what they think," Patrick replied.

"Yeah. I'm not sure what to make of all this, but I'll go with it to appease the kid."

"I just feel bad what happened to his family."

"You mean with his parents splitting up?"

"What? I guess you don't know the story. His father died years ago along with his brother. They drowned in a boating accident right in that river. He ended up coming across his brother's body weeks later."

Eugene looked perplexed. "That's awful. All he ever told me was that his dad was no longer around. I assumed he walked out on his family or his parents divorced."

"No. Why do you think he is the way he is?"

"That makes more sense, although I hate to say it. Man, that's really unfortunate." Eugene said hanging his head.

David called down, "Eugene, can I use your tarp to set up something else? It won't ruin it or anything."

"Sure, kid! Anything you need."

Eugene looked over at Patrick and got back to work.

David came down from the rise and began working on the next component of his ambush. He took the remaining length of rope, tied one end around a stone, then heaved the stone up and over a tree branch above the mud pit. He slowly lowered it down to him and untied the rope, taking it off the stone. He looped the rope through the grommets at the four corners of the tarp and filled it entirely with leaves. While holding on to the rope, he walked back up the rise while raising the filled tarp. David tied it off next to the splintered stump.

After he made sure both ropes were taut, he took a seat for a few minutes and watched everyone below working in his support. Luke, Kelly, and Aaron were walking down the trail checking the other traps. Below him, Patrick gathered leaves to conceal the mud pit, while the drifter delivered yet another heavy bucket of mud.

"This ought to do it," Eugene said.

Patrick scattered leaves over the mud pit. "Looks good to me."

"I didn't realize how many trips that would take, but I'm glad it's done with now. I'm taking a break," Eugene said.

David walked down to meet up with them. "Eugene, thank you," he said. He truly appreciated what Eugene had done for him. The homeless man looked up at the teen with tired eyes and forced a smile. David watched as the shell of a man trudged over to his campsite and flopped down on his sleeping bag. After a minute Eugene called him over.

"What's up?" David asked.

"You know what, David? After what you said the other day about the surveyors trying to take over these woods, I realized you're right. This is our place. I know I talked about moving on, but I'm sick of moving, running on to the next spot. I want to make this town my home and hopefully start doing better for myself. I just hope this is the right place. I'm ready to defend these woods today if things heat up."

David found Eugene's newfound enthusiasm unexpected. The vagrant had been so loyal to him that duping Eugene left David feeling disappointed in himself. But I can't come clean now. I'm too far into this and there's no stopping it. Besides, he'll understand in the end.

"I really am grateful for your help, Eugene." The homeless man grinned and lay back down.

David walked over to Patrick to check up on his progress. "How are things going over here?"

"David, no offense, but what are you going to do if none of this works? Don't get me wrong, the traps are good, but what if these guys get through them somehow? Do you have a backup plan?"

David was already annoyed that Patrick had voiced doubts earlier, but he did not have time to start an argument. "Only thing I can do is just hope this whole thing works," he said. David noticed Luke and his sister waving him down the path to check on something. Aaron stood next to them. David looked at the watch on his backpack and saw that it was almost two o'clock.

Patrick spread out the last handfuls of leaves over the pit and then walked over to Eugene's campsite. "Are you ready for this?"

"I don't know what to think at this point."

"He's even more out of his mind today."

The homeless man closed his eyes to take a nap. "His resolve is no illusion, I'll tell you that much."

CHAPTER 29

At the high school Beth Mathis pulled into a spot closest to the entrance where she normally dropped off David. She parked next to a white car with a peace symbol bumper sticker. She assumed it belonged to Tyler Worthing as it was the only other one in the lot. As she approached the main doors, one of them opened, revealing the guidance counselor. "Right on time," he said checking his watch.

She giggled and walked inside. "Hi, Mr. Worthing."

The guidance counselor gave her a once-over as she walked through the door. "As I said the first time we met, you can call me Tyler, Mrs. Mathis. Please, I insist."

She grinned. "Right."

The two exchanged pleasantries as they walked down the hallway.

When they arrived at his office Tyler Worthing tried to stay casual to hide his nervousness about what he had to reveal. Beth Mathis sat down in the guest chair as he pulled his chair around the desk to sit side by side with her. The counselor relegated the recliner back to being a file holder pushed against the wall. "I'm so glad you could make it down here today. I know this is a strange time to have a meeting with school personnel."

Beth smiled nervously. She still did not understand why Mr. Worthing would hold a meeting on a Saturday. "Sure, no problem."

"Well, David and I have been making some progress, and I wanted to go over some things with you. When I first started these sessions with your son, he was very reluctant to volunteer any information. I would be doing most of the talking trying to get any thoughts or feelings out of him."

"That's David. He tends to do the same thing to me when I try talking to him sometimes."

179

"He would give a little, but that was probably only to throw me a bone every once in a while to give me an inkling that something might be coming. That was his way of holding me at bay. It seemed he might have been more inclined to attend these sessions to get out of class."

"He's a much smarter boy than he lets on."

"I agree he is. He had me going for a while. A few occasions he was late, while at other times he would take long breaks. I realize you do not know me all that well, Mrs. Mathis, but I like to get into the heads of my pupils. Find out what is eating at them and help them fix whatever that is. I like for them to look at things in a different way so that they can view the situation from a perspective other than their own. The last two times we met, David opened up a lot more than I expected."

"Really? How so?"

"Before I get into that, let me first start by saying that I believe you have a wonderful boy in David. Sure he has had his troubles with school, but I can tell he's a good kid. I really feel I can help your son, Mrs. Mathis."

Beth sat back in her chair, feeling a little relieved. She sensed that the counselor was not going to blindside her with any crushing news during this meeting. "Well, I appreciate that, Tyler. David has been through a lot in his young life. More than some people go through in a lifetime."

"Do you want to come with me to the teacher's lounge? Maybe grab a refreshment and then we'll review my findings? They have some refreshments in the fridge and since no one is here, we can have our pick."

"Sure." As they walked down the hallway, Beth asked, "Do you find there is a lot of trouble at this school? I mean, as the guidance counselor, you probably hear about any student issues that are brought to the school's attention."

Tyler pursed his lips, thinking before he spoke. "Well, I do hear a lot, but I have my restrictions and can't look into everything, even though I would like to. It's just impossible to delve into every situation, for many reasons." Beth looked at him expectantly. "For instance, Beth – may I call you Beth?"

"Sure," she said with a shrug of the shoulders.

The counselor smiled and continued. "Just the other day it was brought to my attention through the school administration that there might be a situation this weekend. A fight, perhaps. Now, I have no way of knowing if something is happening or not, as we did not get any specifics, such as the people involved or the place. We are restricted from getting involved in anything that happens outside these school walls because of legal reasons. How it usually works is that our hall monitors or teachers hear rumors from kids gossiping with each other. We try to piece it together if we can."

"Do kids themselves ever come forward with information about issues?"

"That does occur, but very rarely. The school employee usually advises the administration who inform the appropriate channels, be it parents or police. We can act on it in school if we find that we absolutely know who was or is going to be involved in any nefarious activity. If we feel that any future event can be prevented, we surely conduct our due diligence."   "So, the school does not get involved unless it has to?"

"The school can only intervene if the situation occurs on school property or we feel we can thwart something from happening if we know the parties involved. It's kind of viewed like this – just because they go here doesn't mean we're responsible for all facets of their social life."   Tyler's last comment annoyed Beth and it showed on her face as they reached the teachers' lounge.

"What kind of beverage would you like, Beth?"

"Any diet soda is fine, thank you."

The guidance counselor took two sodas from the fridge. "Look Beth, I'm not saying we don't have our students' best interests in mind, because we do. We just can't overstep our boundaries for legal reasons. We live in a litigious society. Believe me, I know."

I wonder what that's about, thought Beth uneasily as they walked back to his office. Tyler patted her on the shoulder and slid his hand down her back in a flirtatious manner. "Please don't worry too much about it. I promise you that I will guide David and help him make the best decisions possible. He is in good hands with me." Beth nodded and stepped away from his touch. The counselor looked away to conceal his discouragement.

Tyler came to a decision on how he was going to divulge what had transpired during the last two meetings. He could not bring himself to give full disclosure, but knew that he had to tell her something since David had the tape in his possession. What I am about to tell her about the thoughts in his head will hopefully make the sleeping agent and hypnosis seem insignificant, he thought. He would just have to hope that the tape never materialized.

At his home, John Gavin sat in his recliner with a beer, playing with a piece of folded up paper in his hands. He had not gotten much sleep the night before thinking about the situation David Collie was in. Here's this loner that no one at school respects, and those two idiots are using him as a guinea pig for some harebrained exercise, he thought as he took a sip from his bottle. The hall monitor sat wondering if he should somehow intervene, knowing full well that the principal was a vengeful man. He had seen the administrator terminate others throughout the years, smearing their names in the process, when they had challenged him.

John Gavin had heard the whispers in the hallways about a showdown between Brock and David sometime soon, possibly this weekend. Yet, like other school employees, the institutional regulations forbade them from getting involved in any outside incidents. He could call the police, but not having any details, only speculation, he did not know when or where the fight might take place.

Between the kids at school in general, Brock, and now the meetings with the counselor, the old hall monitor could not help but feel for David. The thought of the boy being tortured any more than he had been already really ate at him. After another moment of deliberation, he thought, Screw this. I'll just make the call. He unfolded the paper to reveal David Collie's home phone number. He picked up the phone and started to dial the number, but then promptly hung up before it rang. I have to think of how I want to phrase this. Once he was confident in what he wanted to say, he dialed again and waited for someone to pick up.

At the Mathis house, Steve was getting supplies out of the garage. He peeked his head out, hearing the faint ring of the phone from inside the house. "Ah, if it's important they'll call back."

John Gavin let the phone ring a few more times and then hung up, disappointed to not be able to speak with someone. Maybe I'll try again later. Then again, I don't know. It could be a really dumb idea to get involved in the first place. He took another sip of his beer and shook his head, second-guessing himself.

CHAPTER 30

Down at The Shadows, Eugene had just woken up. He rubbed his eyes and looked over at Patrick. "This should be an interesting day. If it turns ugly like David thinks it might, we could be going up against a bunch full-grown men with only a couple of teens and me on our side. I know you guys love these woods, but if some surveyor gets caught up in those traps, it's not going to be pretty. I took down the ones I had protecting my area just in case after I first met David. My traps would just give someone pain and a nice welt. His are serious if they work out the way he has planned."

Patrick thought for a minute. He felt bad that David was duping Eugene in order to get back at Brock. He thought about telling the homeless man the truth, but was sure David would react badly. "I don't know. I feel for David. First time I met him, he was down here alone playing around. He was running around the place like he was hiding from someone, talking nonsense. Who knows? Maybe there were others down here, but no one that I could see."

"I've seen that act myself."

"I was coming back from hanging out down by the river having a few smokes. He almost ran into me, and I nearly scared him half to death. After that I saw him down here a few more times and we started to hang out a bit. I felt bad for the dude, like I should talk to him. Sometimes you can just tell when somebody needs a little interaction to do them good."

Eugene looked over at David who was well out of earshot. "Yep, I know what you mean. I would watch him running around when I first got settled in these woods. He was always off in his own little world talking to whoever. He had no idea I was even here until recently. Kid kind of warmed up to me. I guess with us both being outsiders, he thought he could trust me. What happened to his father and brother, like you told me, was bad enough for him to go through. Now this bullying nonsense..."

"I kind of know what he went through. My sister died up on the railroad tracks years ago. I was messed up for a while, but not like this."

Eugene looked over at Patrick with sad eyes about to say something until they were both distracted by David. He looked to be motioning for his friends to huddle up, calling out their names.

Up the path, David gathered his helpers around him. "I have to run a quick errand," he said.

"What do you want us to do while you're gone?" Luke asked.

"Just make sure the path is clear of any debris and gather more rocks to throw. After that maybe see if Eugene and Patrick need any help." David saw a figure walking towards him on the trail. As the person drew nearer, he smiled. "Hey, Michelle. What are you doing here?"

"Hi, David. I sensed something wasn't right, so I figured I would come find you. What's going on?"

"What is she doing here?" Aaron sneered.

David put his arm out in front of his surly friend. "Relax, Aaron."

"Hello to you as well, Aaron," Michelle shot back.

She turned to David. "Something seems off. What are you up to down here? Not more trouble, I hope."

David shuffled his feet. "Listen, Michelle, everything is fine. I know what I'm doing."

"I don't know, David. I don't like the looks of this. I think we need to talk."

"There is nothing to talk about. I'm fine."

"Just leave, Michelle, you prude." Aaron chimed in.

"I wish you would just talk with me, David," Michelle pleaded.

"Not this time. It's gone on too long. It needs to end."

"I hope you know what you're doing." Michelle shook her head sadly as she turned away. David watched as she faded into the brush. When she was out of sight, the teen went back to briefing his accomplices, gesturing towards the pit as he walked down the path.

"Eugene, Patrick, I was just telling these guys that I have to run an errand. Heading up to the store to use the phone and check in with my mom. These guys can help out with anything you need."

Eugene and Patrick looked at each other. "Okay, David," Eugene said. David walked up the hill to retrieve his bike. Patrick turned to the homeless man.

"I'm not sure what to make of this."

Eugene shrugged. "Your guess is as good as mine."

Back in the guidance office, Tyler Worthing eased into the conversation with Beth Mathis. "So, as I was saying before, at first I was not really getting anywhere with David. Principal Mitchell is very…passionate, we'll say, about his students' well-being. He wants to be sure all his pupils are cared for and safe. When he sees some of them start to go astray he wants to reach out."

"So, do you do this kind of counseling with other students as well?"

With David being the test subject for the principal's experiment, the counselor knew he could not be fully truthful with the woman before him. "Sort of. With David it took a few sessions and a lot of patience to get him to open up, but when he did, it was eye-opening."

Beth was a little baffled. "Okay, but my son doesn't just open up to people. He barely talks to me about anything serious, and I'm his mother."

Tyler shifted in his seat to lean closer to Beth and tried to think of a way to broach the subject. "Beth, we really wanted to help David since things have not been going his way. His grades aren't the best, teachers say he is removed, and he's been bullied both in and outside of school. I know that you are aware of some of these things, but we are on top of it."

The look on Beth's face told him he had her in a vulnerable state. "One day he was in here and wasn't feeling great, so I gave him some over the counter medicine to settle his stomach. It made him a little drowsy, but it also helped relax him."

"Why would you give my son medicine without my permission?"

Tyler reacted quickly. "I do apologize, Mrs. Mathis, but believe me, once you hear what I found out, that will seem trivial. In his sleepy state he began to talk. He started to tell me things." Beth's eyes opened wide at this revelation. "I have to be honest, I'm not happy about what you did, but I need to hear what you found out. I am trusting you, Mr. Worthing."

"Again, I apologize. But I promise you, what I am about to tell you is significant to your son's mental health." Beth looked around the room, trying not to make eye contact with the counselor, and shook her head as her eyes filled with tears. She was angry that this man had seemingly drugged her son, but she was desperate. She needed to know what he had found out, no matter what means he had used to get it.

The rubber tires of David's bike coasted along the asphalt streets as he took his time getting to his destination. There's no turning back now. Everything is set in motion. David stopped on the cracked sidewalk that led to Post's Corner Store. A few people walked in and out as he waited for the opportune time to make his move. A man exiting the store caught his attention. He reminded David of his father. David watched the man, his eyes following him to his car. The man drove off, snapping the boy out of his trance. "Focus, David, focus," he said to himself.

He waited a couple more minutes until the store was vacant except for the clerk. David checked the town clock, which sat in the middle of the street on a concrete island. He still had at least a half-hour. Suddenly a kid stepped out from behind a payphone stand and placed his hands on the bike's handlebars.

"Collie, what the heck are you doing? Getting a pre-fight snack?" The kid laughed as he released his grip on the bike. The three other teens following him snickered. David said nothing. "You better get down there soon, Collie. A lot of people are coming to see this." The teens walked into the store and headed for the video games in the back.

David made his move to the payphone, as he could not spend any more time waiting. He dropped in a quarter, dialed, and listened as the phone rang. No one picked up on the first four rings, which prompted David to end the call rather than waste a quarter. He retrieved the quarter from the return slot and put it back in, dialing once again. After two rings he heard Steve's voice on the other end, breathing heavily.

"Hello?" David froze. "Hello? Who's there?"

"Steve?"

"Your mother isn't home, David."

The teen knew he had to press on with his plan and put on his best panicked voice. "Steve, help me, please!" David's heart beat fast as he spoke, his adrenaline increasing. "I'm up at Post's and this creepy guy has been following me. I don't know what to do."

"Wait. Slow down, David. What's he doing now?"

"He's coming after me right now! Steve, you have to help me!" David hung up the phone. Taking a breath, he walked calmly into the store and approached the teenage clerk. "Hey, man."

The clerk looked up from his reading skater magazine, annoyed at the interruption. "Yeah?"

"Can you do me a favor? My stepfather is going to come up here in about ten to fifteen minutes. If he comes inside looking for me, just tell him I went down to the woods, okay? He'll know why."

"Sure, dude. No problem."

"Thanks." David walked back outside and grabbed his bike. Here we go, he thought.

CHAPTER 31

Beth took a few deep breaths as Tyler moved in a little closer. "Okay, just tell me," she said in a somber tone. The counselor went around his desk and opened the drawer containing his leather-backed notepad. He sat back down, leaning back in the chair and flipped open the pad. He took a half-minute to quickly scan the first few pages, deciding where he wanted to start.

"When David was in that trance, I tried talking to him. Something must have clicked, because he started talking…well, rambling really. When I probed, he talked about everything from your family tragedy to present day struggles he's encountering."

Beth sat up straight. "Wait a second. A trance? What was going on in this office? We are talking deep stuff here if he brought up my late husband and Sam. He never, and I mean never, would talk about that with just anyone."

The counselor chose his words carefully, trying not to implicate himself more than he already had. "I am not an expert in hypnosis. I just figured I would make an attempt to get some type of response while David seemed open to it. I didn't know it would be to this degree."

"I don't know how I feel about all this. You never said anything about this type of method in our meeting, Mr. Worthing." Beth shook her head. The counselor knew he had to get her more intrigued by the information rather than the means by which he had extracted it.

"I'm sorry, but I swear it was safe."

Once he saw she had calmed somewhat the counselor continued. "Let me ask you this, Mrs. Mathis. Do you know of a boy named Luke who your son has been hanging out with recently?" Beth shook her head. "Okay, how about Patrick or Eugene?" Beth again shook her head.

"As embarrassing as it is to admit, I don't know any friends of David's."

"Well, that's okay. As you said, he does not open up much. I only ask because these names came up most in the sessions. At times what David said was gibberish, but he spoke of several notable occurrences. For instance, I have it written right here that he told me about going out with this Luke person late one night. They went to someone's house and threw a brick through the window."

"Oh, my. I cannot even imagine him doing that."

"The problem is, I don't know if it really happened or not. He mentioned that Luke goes to this school, but the only Luke, or in this case Lucas, we have enrolled here is in a wheelchair." Beth looked down at the floor, trying to comprehend what she was hearing.

"Mrs. Mathis, I believe your son is experiencing some major mental issues right now. Maybe it's the bullying or a combination of stressors bringing them on, but I think he needs professional help. I do not believe any of the acquaintances he has talked about are real people. It seems they are illusions or hallucinations he's having."

Beth looked up at him, holding back tears. "Please go on. I want to hear it all."

The counselor realized he was sitting across from a defeated woman as her acceptance of this news explained why she was not getting angry. The fact that Beth did not have any questions about these presumed figments of her son's imagination concerned Tyler. Just as he had assumed, the means by which he attained the information was inconsequential compared to his findings.

Tyler flipped through more pages, trying to explain everything as tactfully as he could while being thorough. "We have been getting some reports that your son has been having conversations with himself in the hallways. I think these conversations might be with these "friends" I listed – Luke, Patrick, and etcetera. I cannot say for sure, but I would venture to guess he has some kind of delusional mental illness brought on by major trauma."

Beth's eyes started to fill up with the obvious insinuation of the family accident. On top of everything else she had heard, it was just too much. "Go ahead, I'll be fine. The accident is just something that I may never get over."

"Okay. I apologize. I know this is a lot to take in." Tyler nervously scratched his temple. I can't believe she wants to continue. It was always hard for him to present tough information to a parent, but this was on a different level. "Maybe the anxiety of being bullied has gotten to him, or maybe it's just everything that he has experienced in his life bubbling up." He looked at Beth. She sat there, not appearing overly upset.

"What were some other names he mentioned?" she asked.

Her question caught the counselor off guard. "Excuse me?"

"Were there any other names?"

Tyler perused his notes. "Well, the names that I caught were Patrick, Eugene, Luke, a Mitchell or Michelle and…Oh, and Aaron. Sorry, I missed that one. When he spoke about other kids he did not give names or I couldn't understand what he was saying."

Beth sat up in her chair, alarmed. "Wait, what was that last name you said?"

The counselor looked down at his booklet again. "Aaron. I have written down here that he said he would speak to this Aaron on the phone."

Beth hung her head in disappointment. "No, no, not again."

"What do you mean, Mrs. Mathis? Who's Aaron?"

Beth composed herself before she spoke. "This is not the first time David has gone through something like this. It has never been this elaborate with all of these names being thrown around, but he has had issues before." She tried to suppress a nervous giggle in between speaking. "This Aaron person is one of David's imaginary friends who came into the picture soon after he found his brother's body, or so one of his counselors told me many years ago. David has been in counseling before, so what you have told me comes as no real shock. I just assumed that things had gotten better, but the recent events seem to have triggered this again."

"When I had David see both a psychologist and psychiatrist before, the name Aaron kept popping up. David talked about him as if he were real. Every time he would do something bad or act out, this Aaron would always be involved. One day David told me that Aaron had moved away, and after that my son seemed to get better. But we have been going through some issues at home lately, especially with his stepfather."

The counselor sat there dumbfounded. "Mrs. Mathis, excuse my bluntness, but why didn't you tell me this before or stop me while I was explaining to you what I had found out?"

Beth looked up with tears in her eyes. "I just needed to hear someone else say it to actually accept it myself. I guess I thought it was just a phase the first time. I was hoping this was all behind us, but now... I don't know what else to do. The last thing I want is for my son to be put in a mental institution. I can't lose another one. I guess I was praying that these sessions would make a difference."

The counselor got up from his chair and tried to console Beth as she wept. "Until this country starts taking mental health more seriously, people like your son will continue to languish. It's not fair." He leaned over and patted her hand. Beth pulled some tissues from her purse.

Tyler looked pensive. "So, he's had imaginary friends in the past... Perhaps he has dissociative identity disorder. That's commonly known as multiple personality disorder. Have you ever heard him talk about any friend that is a positive influence that helps him make good decisions? There could be two or more distinct personalities that can control his behavior."

193

"No, nothing like that. I don't recall hearing of one that counteracted the other. Just this Aaron."

CHAPTER 32

David rode his bike onto the dirt trail as he re-entered The Shadows. He pumped his legs, pedaling hard as his bike rattled over the hard roots and stones. When he arrived at the site, everyone had finished setting up all the traps. David walked down the path, inspecting the setup one last time. He called out to his accomplices. "Everyone gather round."

Eugene, Patrick, Luke, Kelly and Aaron encircled him. "I just want to thank everyone for their help today. I'll see you all after this is over." David checked the watch on his bag and saw that it was nearing three o'clock. "Now let's get into position."

Before retreating back to his campsite, Eugene patted David on the back. "You be careful son. These surveyors are grown men you're dealing with." Again, David felt bad that he had to lie to Eugene, but knew the homeless man would understand the real reason soon enough. He looked around to make sure everyone hid out of sight and waited until Eugene was safely back at his encampment.

He took a deep breath as he walked up the hill out of the woods into the open field. Some kids had already started to gather, and they pointed as they saw him emerge from the brush. He tried to ignore them, but felt their eyes trained on him from a distance. It seemed like a very long walk across the field to the treatment plant steps. David sat down to wait for Brock's arrival.

Steve pulled into the convenience store lot and came to a screeching halt across two parking spots. He leapt out of the car, not bothering to turn it off, as his head was on a swivel looking for the perverse man David had talked about. Not noticing anybody suspicious, he rushed into the store, flinging open the door.

The clerk recognized Steve's urgency. "Easy, bro, watch the door."

"Have you seen a young high school kid with brown hair hanging around outside on a bike a little while ago? Possibly in trouble? Maybe a man lurking around as well?"

The clerk looked confused. "There are a lot of high school kids that hang around the store."

Steve intensely stared at him in response to the smart remark.

"Uh, but, there was a younger dude here who told me someone would show up looking for him. I'm guessing that's you, right?"

The clerk's apathy annoyed Steve. "Right, right, that's me. What did he say? What happened?"

"Calm down, chief. The kid seemed fine, maybe a little weird. All he said was to tell you that he went down to the woods, but that was it. I didn't notice any adult out there harassing him or nothing like that." Steve pounded his clenched fist on the counter. He aggressively yanked open the door, causing it to slam against the interior wall.

"You're welcome, pud," the clerk said under his breath, watching Steve get into his car.

Steve sat back in the driver's seat and tried to make sense of the situation. What is going on here? Either the clerk never saw the man pestering David or David is playing some kind of prank on me, he thought. He slammed both hands on the steering wheel a couple of times in aggravation, trying to decide what to do. I have to go to the woods to make sure he's not in trouble, as much as I doubt that little punk.

Steve sped down the street, coasting through stop signs until he reached a street that ran by The Shadows. He slowed down and canvassed the area in his car first, hoping to hear or see something that would give him a clue to where David might be. After not detecting anything he parked, walked across the silent street and pushed his way through the brush into the woods.

"Where is David now?" Tyler asked.

Beth hesitated, trying to remember what her son had told her in the morning. "Uh, let me think…He mentioned something about going out with some friends. I should have known better, but I was hoping he was starting to become a normal teenager."

The counselor leaned forward in his seat. "Mrs. Mathis, I simply thought that they could be figments of his imagination, but to him they are real. Listen, he still could be interacting with some real people, and I could be wrong. Did he say where he was going?"

"Not really, but he always goes down to the woods even though I asked him to stay away from there. Are you familiar with The Shadows?"

"I am, but mostly from David's sessions. He did mention frequenting that spot. I have it written here that he meets up with Eugene and Patrick down there from time to time. Maybe those were the friends he was talking about?"

Beth looked at the counselor, slowly shaking her head. "I have no idea who either of them are. I don't know what to think anymore."

Tyler had a funny look on his face as a thought had crossed his mind. "What's the matter?" Beth asked.

The guidance counselor looked at a sticky note on his desk that he had received during the week. "Do you remember when I mentioned that we periodically hear about potential issues outside of school?" Beth's eyes followed him as he stood up and started to pace.

"Yes. Where are you going with this?"

"Well, that rumor about a fight this weekend…I wonder if David's connected to it." Beth covered her mouth with her hand at the thought of her son being in harm's way once again.

———

The counselor continued. "Before we get crazy about this, let's think logically. Usually planned fights take place at areas out of public view. If this does involve your son, perhaps it's at the same place David and Brock got into it before. You said that David was out with friends today, and we both know he frequents that wooded area. Eugene and Patrick, whether real or fake, are connected to The Shadows." The counselor flipped through his notebook again. "Okay, here I have that he was concocting some sort of plan for revenge, but I thought it was just talk at the time. It could be nothing, but this all seems to be too much of a coincidence taking into account the trouble between David and Brock lately."

Beth, now shaking, grabbed her purse. "Well, I have to get down there. I can't just sit here."

Tyler came around his desk and gently took hold of Beth's arm, stopping her. "Mrs. Mathis, let me take you there. If it is what we think it is, I have no problem stepping in. I know professionally I should not be getting involved, but I can't let you go alone being how emotional this is for you."

"You're probably right. I would really appreciate that. Thank you."

The two rushed down the hallway and out the school's double doors.

CHAPTER 33

There have to be at least fifty kids here so far, and counting, David thought. The congregation of teens shuffled about in order to catch a glimpse of David sitting on the plant steps amidst the objects he had strategically placed. He looked down at the ground and grew nervous, as he knew this event would start any minute. Just then the crowd shifted and started to clamor.

Brock walked onto the field wearing a cut-off flannel shirt and listening to a Walkman, flanked by Sean and Joe. He pointed at David as the assembled students followed the three boys towards the water treatment plant.

"Here we go!" a random voice yelled out. David chuckled to himself, thinking of how ignorant and emotionless these people had to be to come watch this charade. Brock halted, pushed the stop button on the Walkman, and hung the headphones around his neck. He spit in his hands, rubbing them together while glaring at David. He came into this fight knowing he had to gain back the respect he had lost.

"Come outta there, Collie. It's time." David stood and moved behind his barricade as the three teens advanced towards him. The crowd that had swollen to almost seventy students surged around the trio.

"All right, Brock, we're going to settle this, but I just want to let you know what a worthless piece of crap you are. You pick on people all the time and no one ever stands up to you. Well, that's about to change," David said.

Brock rolled his eyes as Sean and Joe laughed. "Yeah, yeah, Collie. Enough of the speech. Now come out here and get what you have coming to you." The bully handed his Walkman over to Joe and continued on.

David cocked his head and gave Brock a sharp look. "Maybe you're going to get what's coming to you, Brock."

Sean, with a skeptical look on his face, leaned towards Brock. "Something doesn't feel right."

Brock ignored him and moved in closer. "Collie, get out here or else I'm dragging you out from behind that trash heap."

David smirked as he glanced down at the pipe, his emergency weapon that sat inside the large tire to his right. He looked back up at Brock. "Oh, yeah, well why don't ya just try it."

Brock looked around angrily at Joe and Sean who nodded their heads. This kid is not going to make me look bad again, Brock thought. He glanced over his shoulder at the large crowd, then started to trudge forward, determined to pull David from his hiding spot. When Brock reached the blockade, David backed off a little, leaving just enough room to give Brock the chance to grab him.

Brock moved to his left and then his right looking for the best opening to get at David, who remained calm and still. Brock let out a grunt and lunged forward, reaching for David between the large tire and the stacked wooden pallets.

The maneuver startled David and he hesitated enough for Brock to grab hold of his sleeve. David struggled to get free, but Brock had a tight, strong grip on him. The blockade swayed from the force of the struggle, nearly toppling over. The crowd drew closer and some people laughed at the ridiculous spectacle. Sean and Joe approached as well, not wanting to miss any of the beating Brock was about to give his nemesis. "Get him!" Joe yelled with a snicker.

David strained to his right for the pipe that sat in the tire when he heard his shirt start to tear. Suddenly, his sleeve ripped away completely from the rest of his shirt and David fell to the ground. He saw Brock's hand still flailing, trying to get another hold on his prey. David attempted to crawl away, but felt a pull on the back of his shirt. He was able to retrieve the pipe from the tire and then hesitated thinking, Do I really want to go through with this? It's the only way out.

"He's got something," Sean called out as he saw the glimmer of the metal pipe in David's hands.

"What?" Brock said.

Sean pointed at David. "It's Collie! He has something! Watch out!"

Brock could barely hear Sean over the noise of the boisterous crowd. David stood up quickly and swung the pipe down hard on Brock's elbow. The bully yelled in pain and stumbled backward from the barricade, holding his arm. David threw the pipe down and sprinted towards the woods. Here goes, he thought.

Brock pointed after David and yelled at Sean and Joe. "Well, don't just stand there, you idiots. Go get him!" They took off at a run. Brock shook his arm a few times to alleviate the pain and then joined the pursuit, trailing Sean and Joe by a good margin. He turned and yelled to the crowd, "Don't worry! We're bringing him back here!" The mob of students roared their approval.

Tyler's car idled at the red light at the major intersection in the middle of town. Beth was trying to hold herself together. "I don't know what we're going to find, Tyler."

The counselor reached over and took her hand. "Beth, there's no sense in getting worked up. It could be nothing. Maybe he's just there by himself hanging at his usual spots or not even down there at all. We are basically working on a hunch."

Beth look confused. "What do you mean, his usual spots? How would you know what his usual spots are?" Tyler realized he had just slipped up. He let go of her hand. "Tyler, I asked you a question." The counselor hit the gas as the light turned green.

"As part of my research for sessions with David, I did some reconnaissance. I followed him to the woods on a few occasions, just to see what made him tick."

"You mean to tell me you were stalking my son?"

"I…I wouldn't call it that. I just like to know as much as I can about the people I am trying to assist. I was only trying to help him."

Beth looked out the window shaking her head. "First, you tell me that you basically drugged my son and now this?"

"I know it sounds strange, but it really was purely research. You have to understand that I had your son's best interests in mind." He gripped the steering wheel and stared at the road. "Please, I cannot afford to lose another job."

Beth stiffened. "What do you mean? Mr. Worthing, tell me right now!" Tyler groaned inwardly, knowing he should have kept his mouth shut.

"Beth – Mrs. Mathis – it's going to sound worse than it actually was." Beth clenched her hands in her lap. "First let me say that the reason I became a guidance counselor was to help kids." He took a deep breath.

"I had a terrible childhood. My mother was an alcoholic, and my dad left us when I was twelve. I knew that when I grew up, I wanted to have a job where I could help young people who were having a hard time. Working as a counselor in a high school seemed like the perfect fit. I'll admit that I tend to get wrapped up in my students' lives, but that's just because I'm looking out for them."

"What do you mean by 'wrapped up'?" Beth asked.

"Well, one student at a former school I worked at complained that I followed him in my car a couple times, but I was just making sure he got home from school safely during a particularly rough week. It was a bullying situation not too much unlike David's. Unfortunately, his parents claimed I overstepped my bounds, and the administration forced me to resign. That was four years ago."

"How long have you been at Jefferson?"

"Two years," Tyler said quietly.

"So where were you the other two years?"

The counselor did not answer at first.

"Mr. Worthing, I asked you a question. Where were you those two years?"

"Ridville High School over in the western part of the state."

"And what happened there?"

"I was mentoring a young lady with academic and self-esteem issues. It was purely professional, but apparently she told her friends that we had developed feelings for each other. Rumors circulated and the parents accused me of impropriety. Next thing I know the principal let me go shortly thereafter."

"I see. Well, this…"

"I swear to you, Mrs. Mathis, nothing happened with that girl. I was just trying to help her. Just like I'm trying to help David now."

"I can't say that I fully understand your methods, but I do feel you were honestly trying to help my son. But Mr. Worthing, no more surprises, please."

CHAPTER 34

David stumbled down the dirt path into the belly of The Shadows. He looked over his shoulder and saw Joe with Sean trailing close behind. David purposefully slowed to allow Joe to catch up, until he was only about thirty feet ahead of him. David hopped over the heavy fishing line tied between two tree trunks and jogged over the rocks and thorny brush that lay on the ground after it.

Joe ran at full speed, closing in on David. His right ankle hit the trip wire, snapping it and sending him flying forward, arms outstretched as his feet left the ground. He landed hard, his momentum halted by the jagged rocks and thorns. His face smashed against the rocks, chipping his tooth and cutting open his jaw. Joe lay there semiconscious, arms ripped open and bleeding.

David slowed to a walk and looked back in satisfaction at the success of his first trap. Sean reached the spot where Joe was sprawled out. He bent down and shook him by the shoulder. "Joe! What happened? Get up, man!" Joe could only muster a groan. Sean looked up to see David standing on the path. He patted his friend's shoulder. "I'll be back."

David started to jog again as Sean continued his pursuit. When David came to the second trap, he skirted the covered holes, then slowed down, feigning a twisted ankle. As David shuffled along the path, Sean charged forward. His foot landed on the lip of a divot, causing him to stumble. His right foot then plunged into a hole, and his sneaker hit the bottom of the cavity. The forward momentum of his body snapped his shinbone. Sean thrust his body backward, screaming in agony, causing the jagged bone to tear through the skin of his leg. He fainted from the excruciating pain and fell to the ground limp.

In the distance Steve heard the scream. He moved quickly through the wooded area towards the sound. As much as I doubted it, David must be in trouble, he thought.

David looked back at his second victim with a smile. He glanced around and noticed that his accomplices were nowhere in sight. Why isn't anyone at their station? he wondered. No one is throwing anything like we planned. Down the path, Patrick stepped out from behind a bush.

"Dude, this is bad. Those two are hurting."

"Never mind those jerks. Where's the rest of the group?"

Patrick shrugged his shoulders. "I've been playing along with your plan, but I didn't know it was going to go down like this. It's gotten out of hand."

"This coming from the guy who hit Brock in the head with a rock?" said David.

"That was a mistake. I just wanted to scare those guys off or else you would've been in the hospital. But this is insane! It has to stop!"

David stared at Patrick intensely as he realized his friend was turning against him. But before he could verbalize his thoughts, he heard heavy footsteps up the path. Brock burst into view. David smiled. He could not believe his scheme was finally coming to fruition.

Patrick poked him in the shoulder. "How do you expect to get out of this, David? There are two kids badly hurt back there. Who do you think is going to get in trouble? You will!" The look on David's face told Patrick there was no talking sense into him.

"It became clear to me earlier today that you are on the other side. You betrayed me."

Patrick looked bewildered and started to back away. "What? What are you talking about?" David reached down quickly and in one swift motion grabbed a rock and threw it at Patrick. The rock just missed his head as Patrick retreated into the brush before David could grab another.

Up the path, Brock knelt down next to his friend. "Joe, what happened, man? Did you seriously fall and hurt yourself this bad?" Joe could barely lift his head let alone make much sense with his words. "I can't understand what you're saying. I'll be back for you. Sorry, man, but I gotta get this done," Brock said. He moved on, jogging down the path as Joe laid his head back down, spitting out blood.

Brock noticed how eerily quiet it was. Then the sound of a whimper startled him and he saw the hunched figure ahead. "Sean?" Brock could not believe his eyes. He sprinted over to his companion, now knowing full well that these were no accidents. He skidded to a halt just before the series of holes, almost losing his balance trying to avoid them. He looked down at his incapacitated friend. "What the heck is going on?"

Sean had just regained consciousness. "Dude, this kid is sick. Look at my leg, man!" Brock was nearly speechless after seeing the condition of his allies. He looked back at Joe and then at Sean who sat with his tibia poking out of his skin, groaning. "Okay, okay, man. Don't worry. I'm gonna get that kid." He moved carefully around the holes.

"Don't leave me here, Brock! Who knows what this nut is capable of!" Sean pleaded.

"I'm gonna fix this and then get you guys help." Brock broke into a run, his own agenda overshadowing the welfare of his friends. "It'll be okay, Sean, I swear!"

David reached Eugene's camp and hid behind a tree as he watched Brock make his way down the path. Luke, Kelly and Aaron peeked out from behind a bush. David gestured for them to stay down, and the three of them disappeared back into the vegetation. Eugene came out of his tent. "Is it time? Are the surveyors following you, David?"

"Yes, Eugene, one of them is on his way. Just stay back for now." David ran up the rise that overlooked the campsite and mud pit. He positioned himself by the tree that anchored the two ropes supporting the tarp and the stump.

Brock approached the mud pit and stopped abruptly, now well aware the path was booby-trapped. The pit was not well camouflaged, being sparsely covered by leaves, and he spotted it easily. He looked around for David. "What is this, Collie? Show yourself!"

Eugene appeared from behind a tree and approached the irate teen. Brock looked him over and stepped around the pit, walking closer to the vagrant. "I don't know who you are, and I don't care. I just want to know where David Collie is."

The sight of Brock confused Eugene. He had been expecting to see an adult surveyor as David had told him, not a juvenile. "Who are you, kid? What are you doing here?"

"You look like the kind of weirdo that would help him out with all this. Get out of my way." Brock, already infuriated, tried to push his way past the homeless man, but Eugene grabbed his arm.

"Listen, kid. I don't know what you're doing here, but David has been through enough. All we're doing down here is trying to prove a point. So why don't you just leave."

Brock's eyes grew wide. "So you did help him. This whole thing was a setup. I came down here for a fight and stepped into an ambush."

"What are you talking about?"

"You know exactly what I'm talking about. You deserve this, you dirt ball." Brock cocked his fist and took a swing at Eugene who quickly sidestepped the blow. Brock stumbled forward and then righted himself. They turned to face each other, with Eugene's back to the mud pit.

"What are you doing, kid? I think there's a misunderstanding here."

Brock furrowed his brow. "Then you're in the wrong place at the wrong time. If you know David Collie and helped him, then I'm definitely not the person you wanted to see." Without hesitation Brock charged Eugene. Calling on his military hand-to-hand combat skills, the homeless man assumed a defensive posture. When Brock lunged at him, Eugene took a step forward, grabbing him under the arm. Using Brock's momentum, he hip-tossed the teen into the pit.

His face covered in mud, Brock tried to stand as his legs sank into the muck. Eugene watched him struggle, not sure if he should help the kid who had just attacked him unprovoked. I have to get out of here, Eugene thought.

Watching the action from above, David pulled the rope attached to the tarp. Brock instantly found himself showered by leaves, making it even more difficult to see anything around him as he desperately tried to escape the sludge. "You had this coming to you, Brock," David called down.

Brock attempted to turn in his disoriented state. "Collie? Where are you? When I get out of here, you're dead! You hear me?" Brock continued to wipe away mud from his face to gain his bearings.

Brock's words unfazed David as he grabbed the splintered log to his right. He swung it down at his adversary, trying to mimic the same plane he had practiced. The log sliced through the still-falling leaves towards the vulnerable bully stuck in the mud. David's device whistled past him, close enough that Brock felt the rush of air. "What was that?" he cried.

The log reached the apex of its swing, then the momentum brought it back down toward the trapped teen. On its second pass, the fragmented end of the log caught Brock just below his rib cage, tearing a hunk of flesh away from his body. As the log twisted away, Brock felt the cool air on his open wound and looked down in horror. He fell back without a word, and his blood mixed with the mud as he began to breathe heavily.

Eugene looked on with his hands on his head. "Oh my God!"

On the slope above the pit, David jumped up in triumph, throwing his fist in the air. "Yes!"

Eugene looked up at David incredulously, horrified and confused by what had just played out before his eyes. After a moment of taking it in, the homeless man finally comprehended what had just transpired. David used me. There were no surveyors. This was all just a ploy to get back at this kid. Eugene watched as Brock began to cough up blood.

"David!" Eugene yelled at the teen who was now running down the rise.

Not too far away, Steve heard a strange man shout David's name. He forged on, pushing his way through the shrubbery toward the commotion.

When David made it down to ground level, he looked around for the others but did not see anyone. As David locked eyes with Eugene, he could see the hurt in his face. David knew at that moment that Eugene had figured it out. "I'm sorry," the teen lipped as he ran off into the woods.

Eugene snapped out of his daze and ran back to his campsite knowing he had to leave at once. He gathered all his necessities as fast as possible, not wanting to be anywhere near this place when the police discovered the carnage.

CHAPTER 35

Steve caught sight of David running through the trees. "David!" he shouted.

His stepson waved at him and gestured back toward the campsite. "That's the guy I called you about! I'm going to hide over there!" David nodded towards the river bank by the drainage pipe. If the last part of his plan materialized, Eugene, with his military background, would be able to seriously injure Steve in a fight. Steve is so desperate to be the hero. Still trying to look good for my mom. This is too easy, David thought.

Steve reached Eugene's campsite as the vagrant was finishing packing his essentials. Eugene heard the snap of a twig and, already on edge, whipped around to face Steve. "Who are you?"

Steve clenched his fists and eyeballed the shovel leaning against a tree. "You don't want to know."

"Are you one of the surveyors?" Eugene asked. "Because if you are, I didn't know what that kid was planning down here, honestly." Steve heard a groan and looked over to see a teenager mired in the mud, half-conscious and bleeding profusely. Steve looked aghast at Eugene.

"Surveyors? What the hell is going on down here? What did you do to that kid?"

"Listen, man, that wasn't me. The boy who did it just ran off. He did everything. He lied to me about what was really going on down here."

The situation baffled Steve. "You got some major issues, scum bag. That kid who just ran away is my stepson. He called me about you, said you were hassling him up at the convenience store."

Now Eugene was really mystified. "I've been down here the entire day. I know David and we've hung out many times. Why would he say that? These other kids, I don't even know who they are!"

"What do you mean, 'kids'? There are more?"
Steve had heard enough. "You're pathetic. You expect me
to believe you don't know what's going on?"

Off in the brush, Patrick shook his head, trying to
make sense of it all. He had stuck around to see the
aftermath of the twisted plan that David's mind had
concocted. It was now becoming clear to him why David
had set up this entire scenario. He's manipulated everyone
into taking care of all his problems at once. Patrick walked
away towards the train bridge feeling demoralized, not
being able stomach anymore violence.

"All right, take it easy now. If I don't know David,
then how do I know about his family's accident? His father
and brother drowned in this river. A stranger would never
know something like that about him, right?"

"Everybody in town knows that story. You could
have heard it anywhere." Steve narrowed his eyes. "Look, I
got a call from my stepson saying a man was after him. I
come down here to find him running away and a severely
wounded kid over there. You really expect me to believe
anything you say?"

Eugene knew there was no way to talk to this man
rationally. David had counted on that when he had devised
his plan. Steve suddenly lunged for the shovel. Eugene
reacted and made a grab for the shovel as well, having
nothing else to protect himself from the imposing man.
They collided and crashed into the bushes.

David stood on the pipe looking out on the river,
smiling and thinking about the ruckus he had caused. It's
about time something went my way, he thought. After a
couple of minutes, the commotion at the campsite faded
and he heard footsteps. I'd better make this good if Eugene
is ever going to forgive me. After all, he did take care of
that jerk Steve for me. He forced out some tears to appear
distraught. Then he took a deep breath, waiting for the
homeless man to speak first.

"Hey," said an out-of-breath, familiar voice. David turned, tears standing in his eyes, and froze in shock. His stepfather stood before him on the pipe, dirty from his struggle, wearing a few scratches on his face. "Are you all right, David?"

The guidance counselor sped down the street that ran parallel to The Shadows. Beth Mathis drew a sharp breath as they passed by a parked car. Was that Steve's car? But it can't be. There's no reason he would be down here.

Eugene rolled over and tried to get up, but he could barely stand on his injured leg. In the scuffle, he had been hit in the head with the shovel, and his ears were still ringing. He limped toward the river, following the sound of raised voices, and fell down into some tall grass when he caught sight of his attacker. From the cover of the weeds, Eugene had a clear view of David and his stepfather arguing on the pipe. Eugene's knee throbbed as he reached down and massaged it. A few seconds later he was startled by the sound of a scream and looked back up. The homeless man could not believe his eyes as he saw the water splash. Eugene was speechless as only one person remained standing on the pipe.

The tires squeaked as the guidance counselor's car turned at the corner and then made a hard left in the middle of the block up the access road that led to the water plant. Tyler pulled up next to the "For Sale" sign that David had felled. Beth bounded out of the car, barely waiting for it to stop, and headed for the field crowded with teenagers.

"Beth, wait!" Tyler caught up to her and led her onto the field. Students started to disperse as they recognized the guidance counselor. "Is David Collie here?" Tyler shouted.

"My son! Where is my son?" Beth pleaded.

One student pointed towards the woods. "They chased him down there."

Beth and Tyler reached the rim of the field and entered The Shadows more than halfway down David's booby-trapped trail.

"Help!" Sean called out. Tyler ran up the path to him. The boy's condition sickened him as the counselor looked him over.

"Sean, what happened to your leg!" The boy moaned in pain. Tyler looked up to see Joe staggering toward him, holding his head, blood dripping down his arms. "Oh, my God!" He ran to the boy and supported him as he walked. "Here, you sit with Sean while I get help."

Beth saw a recognizable figure approaching. It was her husband. "Steve, what are you doing here? What's going on? Why are you all wet?"

Steve took her hand with a melancholy look on his face, water dripping from his hair and clothing. "This is bad. I got a call from David that led me down here and I came across this… this massacre. It was complete anarchy. I had to fight off some bum and…I don't know. I am just as confused as you are. As for…" Beth interrupted with a shriek as she saw Brock's lifeless body slumped over in the mud.

Beth grabbed her husband's face. "Where's David? Is he okay?"

Steve hugged his wife and put his chin on top of her head, taking a deep breath. "David's gone. I saw him fall into the river from a drainage pipe back there. I jumped in and tried to save him, but he went under and then…I just lost him. I don't know if he jumped in on purpose or fell by accident. I'm so sorry, Beth." His wife started to sob uncontrollably, nearly collapsing.

As the strong current pulled him downstream David gasped for air. Luke, Kelly, and Aaron waved goodbye to him from the bank. Michelle appeared out of the woods, tears streaming down her face. "Help!" David cried, his one arm reaching out of the river. Then he watched as each of the figures vanished into thin air. He managed to float on his back for a moment and saw Patrick's face staring down at him from the train bridge. "Patrick, help me!" David choked out. He struggled to keep his head above water, flailing his arms and trying desperately to get closer to the bank, but he was just too tired. The water closed over his head as his lungs filled with river water.

CHAPTER 36

After two weeks, Beth Mathis finally mustered the fortitude to go into David's room. The authorities called off the missing person search. David was officially pronounced dead, although his body had not been recovered. Beth opened the door and breathed in the stale smell of the idle room. She walked across the carpet, stumbling over a rotary phone that sat on the floor. What is that doing in here? she thought. There isn't even a phone jack in his room.

She sat on the bed and looked around, taking it all in. David's closet door was ajar. Beth opened the closet and looked through his clothes, pushing them aside one by one. Looking down she pulled back a tattered blanket to reveal a rifle and a shotgun. She recognized Charlie's initials carved on the rifle stock and gasped. Why would he have brought his father's guns up here? I hope he wasn't thinking of using them to...

Beth sank to the floor in despair and sat motionless for a minute. She could not help but wonder what her son's next scheme would be if were alive to fulfill it. She resumed searching the rest of the closet for anything else hidden and noticed a loose panel in the back. Beth pulled the piece of wood away, revealing the secret compartment.

Sitting back on the bed, she took a deep breath and prepared herself as she opened up the box. The first thing she saw was a note sitting atop a cassette tape labeled "David Collie Sessions." Beth placed the cassette off to the side and started reading the note. The first lines filled her with anger and she put the note down, choosing to read the rest later.

Small slips of paper and torn pieces of loose leaf with scrawled writing on them filled the shoebox. Beth was distraught by what her son had written. How much he hated school. Nightmares he had been having. Conversations with friends – Aaron, Michelle, Patrick. Predictions about what would happen to the people around him. Cynical thoughts about other students at school. I'm tired of being picked on. I might have to do something to take care of this, one slip of paper read. The ramblings of an individual in desperate need of help. Beth shook her head and cried, wishing she had known just how mentally ill her son had become.

She put everything back in the box, including the cassette. She could not bring herself to listen to the tape just yet, knowing it was a recording of David's meetings with Tyler Worthing as described by the note. They used my son for an experiment. She put her head in her hands.

The following day Beth went to The Shadows and walked down the trail toward the river. Volunteers filled the holes and mud pit. They also cleared away the debris and the path was smooth. She paused on the trail and looked around. All was quiet except for the calling of some birds. She shook her head, still in disbelief at what occurred here resulting in her son's seemingly suicidal drowning. Why? Beth's eyes started to fill up as she walked out on the pipe by the water and placed three white roses on the edge. She looked out over the choppy river and sighed.

After a few minutes, a voice from behind alarmed her. "Excuse me, ma'am." She turned around to find a disheveled, dirty man staring at her. "Do you want to know what really happened here that day?" he asked.

A little uneasy and confused, Beth walked off the pipe to put herself in a less vulnerable position. "I assume you are the man the police questioned. Listen, I don't want any trouble."

The vagrant shook his head with a fleeting laugh. "I'm harmless, but I can understand your reaction. I must look kinda scary and the police thing…yeah, that really was inevitable. But I had nothing to do with your son falling into that river."

Beth took a deep breath. "My entire family has been taken by that river."

"Yeah, I know about all that and am so sorry. I cannot even imagine your loss. David and I were friends. My name is Eugene."

"You're Eugene? The school counselor told me David talked about you…in a way." Beth felt relief that at least one of the names Tyler had told her was an actual person.

"David was a good kid, and he was kind to me. Well, right up until that last day." Eugene stepped up closer, so close that she could smell his unwashed funk. "That day he tricked me into helping him ambush those bullies. He had told me surveyors were coming to prep these woods for bulldozing. I've been living here for a while, so I had some skin in the game, but mostly I went along with his plan because he loved this place." He chuckled. "David was smart. Had me fooled."

Beth suppressed a smile. "Sorry he did that to you. He sure knew how to fool some people."

"I can't really hold that against him. He was troubled, and people can only take so much before they snap. The day he drowned, he was talking to different imaginary people he thought were helping him...Luke and Aaron and a girl from what I could discern. I just played along because I felt bad for him. I didn't know how else to handle it." Beth closed her eyes. Aaron was a name she was all too familiar with and Luke had come up in Tyler's sessions as well as in the shoebox notes.

Eugene cleared his throat. "I don't think what happened to David was no accident or suicide."

Beth's eyes flew open. "What do you mean?"

"I believe his own stepfather – your husband – pushed him in."

"You're crazy! When I got down here Steve was soaking wet from jumping in to save David. He told me he was attacked by a bum – you! Why would I believe someone like you?" She started to back away.

"Let me talk. Please." Eugene held out his hands in a calming gesture and took a step back. Beth halted.

"I'll start at the beginning. On that day, when I realized David had conned me into helping him set up the traps to hurt those kids, I figured I should scram before the cops came. I was packing up my stuff when your husband ran into my campsite and accused me of hassling David – said he'd gotten a phone call from him. Which makes sense since David went to run an errand before everything started down here."

The lengths her son had taken to set everything into motion to work in his favor that day dumbfounded Beth.

"Then he attacked me. I busted up my knee during the struggle, and he hit me in the head with a shovel." Eugene pointed to the scab on the side of his head. "See? Your husband did that."

Beth stared at the man impassively.

"After he laid a beating on me, he went to David who was standing on that pipe." Eugene pointed over Beth's shoulder. "With the condition of my knee I couldn't make it far, but I headed in the direction of what sounded to be an argument. I flopped down in some tall grass before my knee gave out to hide from your husband and to catch of glimpse of what was happening. I had a view of the two and could hear them yelling at each other, but I could only make out some of what they were saying. One thing was certain, your husband was furious. He was cursing your boy up and down. Saying how David made his life miserable at home. Apparently, David tricked your husband into coming down here to fight me. I guess he thought I could take care of Steve for him."

"Anyway, I took my eyes off of them for a moment and the next thing I know I heard someone fall into the water. Your husband was standing at the end of the pipe yelling at David in the water." Eugene shook his head in disbelief as he recalled the event. "I'll never forget the look on his face. It was pure rage. Then he jumps in himself and gets right back out. I can only guess he got wet so he could lie to you about trying to save your son. He didn't even attempt to." Eugene closed his eyes. "I couldn't run because of my leg, so I stayed hidden until you all left. Later the police did a sweep of the woods and found me. I spent the night in jail because your husband fingered me for what happened to those other kids." He opened his eyes and met Beth's skeptical gaze.

"I tried telling the police the traps were David's doing and that your husband killed your son. But it was my word against his. Why would the cops believe a burned-out bum like me? There was only one cop who didn't think I was crazy – an Officer Keller. He knew of David somehow." Beth looked astounded, recalling the officer's visit to her home. That was the day she had found out about the bullying. "They finally dropped the charges once the surviving boys named David as the culprit behind the ambush."

"Anyway, I've been hoping you would come down here so I could tell you all of this. It's not like I could go knock on your door."

Beth again stood expressionless and quiet.

"Ma'am, really, why would I be telling you all this?" he pleaded. "I have nothing to gain. I just want justice for David."

Beth reached into her pocketbook and brought out her wallet. Her hand shook as she extended it, holding up a picture of her and Steve. "Is this the man you're talking about?"

Eugene nodded. "You know it is, ma'am. The very same guy who was consoling you that day." Beth's knees buckled. Eugene caught her before she fell to the ground and walked her over to sit on the drainpipe. "We need to go back to the police. They didn't believe me, but maybe if both of us go…"

It was silent for a minute as tears slid down Beth's cheeks. "I guess I really cannot say it is that unbelievable."

Then she pushed up her sleeve, revealing a hand-shaped bruise on her upper arm. "He did this. Lately it has been rougher than usual. How could I have not have seen…?"

Beth gathered herself before she continued. "They even came to my house to speak with Steve during the investigation…I guess after you said something while you were at the station. Maybe Officer Keller has something to do with that. But they never even batted an eye questioning his explanation of what happened." Beth hung her head for a moment and then looked up at the homeless man. "I don't know if it's enough."

"We can only try," Eugene said reassuringly.

The two started their walk down the trail on their way out of The Shadows.

Standing behind a tree within earshot of the conversation, Patrick had deliberated about whether or not to approach them mid-discussion, but chose to listen instead. Hanging out near the train bridge almost every day, Patrick had been waiting to see if David's mother would come back to The Shadows. He also had been evading Eugene in the aftermath of the traumatic events.

Even though David was no longer here, Patrick still harbored conflicting feelings up until this point. His friend had gone too far that day, and Patrick was angry that David had affected so many lives in one short afternoon. Did David get what he deserved? he often wondered. But the teen had been more disturbed than any of them had known. Now, after hearing the talk between Beth and Eugene, Patrick knew he had to do what was right and support Eugene's claim to the police. *From the train bridge I saw David's stepdad push him in. I have to put this behind me and tell them.*

Patrick stepped out from his hiding place and yelled, "Hey!"

Beth froze hearing a teenage boy's voice call out. Eugene turned to see a familiar face jogging up the trail. He smiled. "Patrick."

"I think I can help," Patrick said.

At the riverbank, a breeze picked up and the three roses Beth had placed on the pipe fell into the water. They separated as they floated downstream, then came together, drifting as one.

35269439R00126

Made in the USA
Middletown, DE
04 February 2019